THE
CARREFOUR
CURSE

Dianne K. Salerni

HOLIDAY HOUSE · NEW YORK

Library of Congress Cataloging-in-Publication Data

Names: Salerni, Dianne K., author.
Title: The Carrefour curse / by Dianne K. Salerni.
Description: First edition. | New York : Holiday House, [2023] | Audience:
Ages 8–12. | Audience: Grades 4–6. | Summary: "When twelve-year-old
Garnet finally gets to meet her magical extended family she discovers
they're all trapped in the ruins of their crumbling manor and
Garnet must break a curse that has decimated three generations
of Carrefours"— Provided by publisher.
Identifiers: LCCN 2022022151 | ISBN 9780823452675 (hardcover)
Subjects: CYAC: Magic—Fiction. | Dwellings—Fiction. | Inheritance and
succession—Fiction. | Blessing and cursing—Fiction. |
Families—Fiction. | LCGFT: Novels.
Classification: LCC PZ7.S152114 Car 2023 | DDC [Fic]—dc23
LC record available at https://lccn.loc.gov/2022022151

ISBN: 978-0-8234-5267-5 (hardcover)

For Bob, again and always

Crossroad House

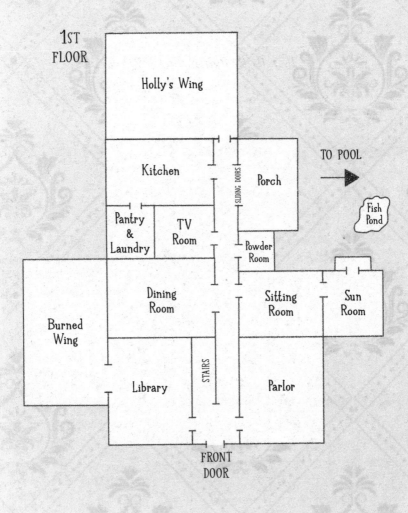

1ST FLOOR

Holly's Wing

Kitchen

SLIDING DOORS

Porch

TO POOL

Fish Pond

Pantry & Laundry

TV Room

Powder Room

Burned Wing

Dining Room

Sitting Room

Sun Room

Library

STAIRS

Parlor

FRONT DOOR

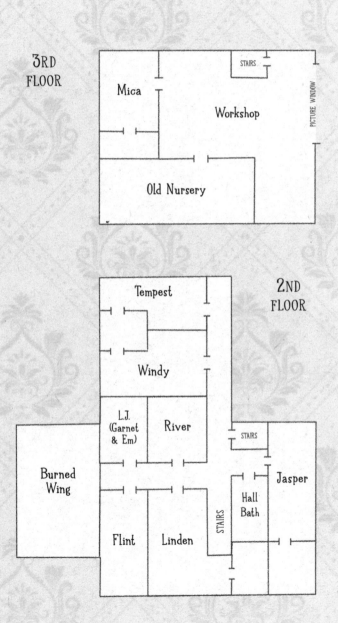

3RD
FLOOR

Mica

Workshop

STAIRS

PICTURE WINDOW

Old Nursery

2ND
FLOOR

Tempest

Windy

L.J.
(Garnet
& Em)

River

STAIRS

Burned
Wing

Jasper

Hall
Bath

STAIRS

Flint

Linden

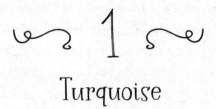

Turquoise

Color: *blue-green, sometimes mottled*

Magical properties: *promotes physical and emotional healing, good health, good fortune, and good travels*

To recharge: *place in direct sunlight*

Y ou'd think spitting up frogs would be a lot like the worst stomach flu you've ever had, but it's surprisingly different. A knot travels slowly up your esophagus and into the back of your throat. It hops onto your tongue, and then *ptooey*, you spit out the frog.

A quiet but disgusting bit of magic.

The frogs, each less than an inch long, haven't yet filled up the basin in my lap, but if I don't get rid of them soon, they'll be hopping around the car. "You have to pull over, Mom."

My mother wrenches her eyes off the road long enough to shoot me a wild-eyed glance. She's taking this harder than I am, which seems strange, but I think it's better if *somebody* remains calm. "Just throw them out the window, Garnet."

"I can't do that!"

"Why not? It's not like they're—" Mom doesn't finish the sentence. She can't tell me the frogs aren't real. Hallucinations don't leave a trail of slime on your tongue.

Which makes me wonder—where are they coming from? Are they magically popping into existence in my stomach? Or are they being frognapped from some peaceful pond and subjected to a situation that is probably as unpleasant for them as it is for me? Either way, I won't throw them out the window of a moving car. "Mo-o-om!"

"Okay, okay!" She puts her blinkers on and pulls onto the side of the road. "Hurry up. The faster we get where we're going, the sooner this will stop." Even now, she avoids saying the name of our destination.

I pop the handle to open my door and tip the frogs onto the shoulder of the road. *Go free, little guys.* I've barely closed the door when Mom peels onto the road again and stomps on the gas. "Use the bracelets I gave you," she says between clenched teeth. "Call upon the power of the stones to control the phenomenon and slow it down."

"I'm trying!" But the bracelets aren't helping.

It's not like Mom's practical magic shop carries amulets specifically for a plague of frogs. One of the bracelets Mom shoved at me during our frantic departure from home is a ringlet of obsidian and turquoise crafted to relieve nausea in pregnant women. The other incorporates a bloodstone to ward off magical danger—but it hasn't stopped this frog curse.

In fact, here comes another one, sliding over the back of my tongue. I spit the frog into the metal basin with a squelchy *pi-i-ng*.

My finger pads stroke the stones in the bracelets, seeking relief. By now I know each one by heart. This oblong obsidian is next to the turquoise with the jagged edge. The bloodstone has a j-shaped chip on its underside. But I can only sense their physical shapes, not their magic.

Actions beget consequences. It's one of the first lessons in magic Mom taught me. And I think I'm paying the price for my actions now. Because not only are the bracelets useless against my affliction, I also can't seem to hear or influence the power of the stones. Me! Garnet Carrefour!

I was named by my mother for a powerful gemstone, and I've been listening to the secret song of stones for as long as I can remember. In fact, it wasn't until I was almost in kindergarten that I understood that other people *couldn't* hear them. Tonight, the silence is deafening. I'm pretty sure I'm being punished for what I did earlier today, but I can't tell Mom about that. Not until we get to Crossroad House.

Her phone starts ringing in the cup holder. I balance the basin on my knees while I check the screen. "It's Holly."

Mom shakes her head, but I stab the green icon anyway. "Hi, Holly. This is Garnet."

"Hello, darling. Is it still happening?"

Darling sounds overfamiliar for someone I've never met, even if she is my mother's cousin. "Yeah, it's still happening."

"What did you do, Holly?" Mom yells in the direction of the phone. "What in the name of earth magic did you and Linden do?"

"Nothing to Garnet!" Holly's voice protests. "We cast a simple summoning spell on *you.* Windy warned you we'd be forced to do that if you didn't come willingly."

"I blocked your spell, so you *must* have cast something on my daughter." The fury in Mom's voice echoes through the car. I would have felt the same if I thought her cousins were to blame for my predicament, but I think I accidentally did this to myself.

"We would never!" Holly exclaims. "And why would we send *frogs*? Bring her to Crossroad House, and we'll see what can be done."

Mom flinches at the name of her childhood home. "That's what I'm trying to do, so stop distracting me." She snatches the phone from my hand and thumbs it off.

Crossroad House. Despite Mom's bad temper and the unpleasantness of the frogs, a shiver of anticipation wiggles down my spine.

I'm finally going to the Carrefour family estate, where my mother grew up. It's only ever been a legend to me, the setting of Mom's stories about her childhood. But I've never seen it. Mom didn't keep any photos when she left—except for one of herself and her cousins lounging beside the pool in their swimsuits and 1990s hairstyles. And she has always *refused* to take me there. Mom hasn't set foot in Crossroad House since before I was born, and she isn't happy about being forced back by a magical parade of regurgitated frogs. She already ignored several hints, refused a request, and attempted to block a summons.

The hints, the request, and the threat of summons all came by way of Windy, another Carrefour cousin. Despite Mom's self-imposed exile from the family home, she and Windy kept in regular contact. A month ago, Windy started pressuring her to come home. This afternoon they had a heated FaceTime call, which Mom made from her bedroom in our apartment over the shop. Because she took the extra step of closing the door for privacy, I took the extra step of eavesdropping at the crack under the door.

Information about Crossroad House is golden.

I was in position in time to hear Windy lay down an ultimatum. "The old man is dying. He insists you and Garnet join the family before that happens."

Before I could get my hopes up that Mom might relent, she retorted, "I'll believe he's dead when I see him in his coffin. And then I'll want to nail the lid shut."

Harsh!

Windy must've thought the same because she exclaimed, "Really, Em! In spite of everything, Jasper *is* your grandfather."

This clarified which old man they were talking about. Because there are two elderly Carrefour men living at Crossroad House, as far as I know.

"Everyone needs to be here for the transition," Windy continued.

"Why? He'll choose Linden as heir. Everybody knows that."

There was a pause before Windy said, "Maybe he'll choose me."

Mom snorted. "Is that why you're pestering me? To gain points with Jasper?"

"I'm calling to warn you. Jasper demands that you be summoned if you won't come, and Holly and Linden have agreed to do it."

Mom's reaction must have been plain on her face because I didn't hear her say anything, but Windy pleaded, "They don't have a choice. You can't blame them."

"I'll blame who I choose." Mom snapped her laptop shut then, and I scooted my butt away from the door, rotating onto my knees once I reached the living room carpet and vaulting over the back of the sofa in front of the TV. When my mother emerged from her bedroom, her expression was angry, but it didn't seem directed at me. "Garnet, fetch a pair of red candles from the shop."

Pretending that I'd been watching TV instead of eavesdropping was easy to do when I was genuinely confused. "*Red* candles?"

White candles are for protection. Red is for...well... battle.

"Red!" Mom said sharply. "And hurry!"

Now—hours later—with me burping frogs and our car careening along a dark New England road toward Crossroad House, Mom mutters to herself. "It should've worked. My ward should have stopped their summons."

Actions beget consequences.

I spit another frog into the basin and don't admit to what I did.

Celestite

Color: *pale white, blue, green, or pink*

Magical properties: *relieves fear of meeting new people, removes negative energy from a room*

To recharge: *place on a clean cloth in indirect sunlight*

The sky is inky dark when Mom brings the car to a halt at the end of a torturous trek down a bumpy dirt road. Crossroad House looms over us, its bulky outline opaque against the indigo sky and broken only by a façade of brightly illuminated windows. I claw at the car door, desperate to enter the house if that will bring this curse to an end.

Did I say I was calmer than Mom? Not anymore. My throat is sore, and my stomach keeps revolting, although nothing but frogs comes up with each retch. I've been clutching the bracelets for the last hour and a half, whispering the words of a spell.

"I call upon the strength of obsidian and the spiritual energy of turquoise to heal me. Beautiful, spotted, generous bloodstone, cast off this curse!"

Contrary to what people think, there are no rhymes in real magic. No *double, double, toil and trouble.* (Sorry, Shakespeare.) Magic works best when you tell the elements of your spell exactly what you want from them. Flattery helps, too. But tonight I might as well be blowing out birthday candles.

I defied Mom this afternoon because I wanted to visit Crossroad House. And yes, I knew that what I did made me a target. But being cut off from my magic? I did not count on that.

At first it was like the numbness of a hand after you've accidentally slept on it all night. But that wears off. It doesn't spread throughout your body the way the loss of magic has spread through mine. Snaking through my limbs and seeping into my hands and feet like poison. What if the feeling—the magic—never comes back? What if I unknowingly sacrificed it when I committed my act of minor rebellion?

I can't make my hands operate the car door, but someone outside yanks it open for me. I fall out, dropping my basin of frogs, only to be caught by two men. "Be careful with her!" Mom shouts.

"Of course, Em!" one of them calls back. Grasping me under the armpits, the men lift me off my feet and haul me up a set of concrete steps.

At the top, a woman with tan, wrinkled skin and steel-gray hair holds the front door open. "So this is Emerald's child," she says, frowning as if she's not sure she likes what she sees.

I vomit a cascade of frogs over the threshold.

"Well!" The woman stands aside so I can be carried into the house. "I see her condition was not exaggerated!"

The men cart me into a room filled with people. I wanted to meet my relatives, but not like this! My stomach heaves as another knot of froggy flesh pushes its way up my esophagus.

My mother bursts in behind me. "We did what you wanted. We're here! Why is it getting worse?"

"Em, this isn't our doing!" A plump woman with pink cheeks and a head full of strawberry-blond curls places an ancient-looking leather-bound book on a large wooden desk. "Bring her over here!"

The men plop me into a chair and push it over to the desk. I lean over the armrest and barely miss someone's shoe with the next frog barf. People back away quickly, although they all gather in a semicircle across the desk from me, staring like I'm a vaguely disgusting zoo exhibit.

"That's wicked nasty," says a teenage girl with dark, spiky hair and a nose ring.

Tell me about it.

The woman with the wild curls thrusts the book open. I expect a cloud of dust, but the giant tome is immaculately clean. Maybe even *magically* clean.

This must be the Family Book. It's a record of the Carrefours dating back to the 1700s. More than that, it's a contract that binds new Carrefours to the family magic. I've heard about it from Mom, but this is my first glimpse of the book itself. The woman leafs through the pages until she finds what she wants: a family tree with six generations, stemming from the original Linden Carrefour, the man who built Crossroad House.

Family Tree

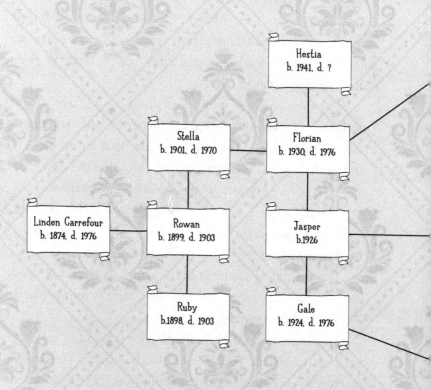

Hestia
b. 1941, d. ?

Stella
b. 1901, d. 1970

Florian
b. 1930, d. 1976

Linden Carrefour
b. 1874, d. 1976

Rowan
b. 1899, d. 1903

Jasper
b.1926

Ruby
b.1898, d. 1903

Gale
b. 1924, d. 1976

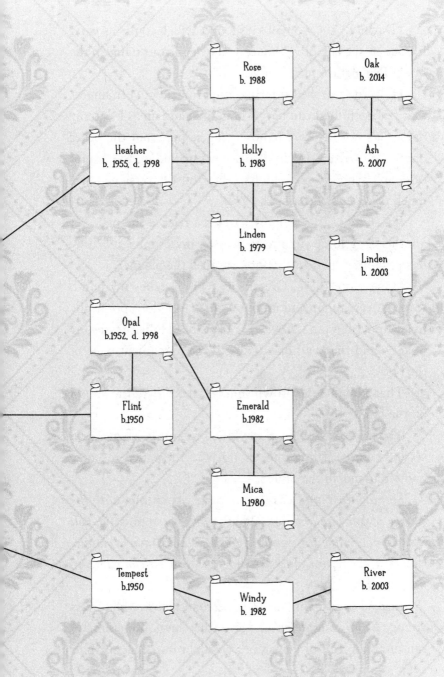

"Darling," the woman says to me, which confirms what I thought: she is Holly. "I need you to sign your name in the book. I've made a place for you."

I take the pen she's offering, fumbling it between fingers that feel nothing. I can barely hold my hand up as I sign my name. It's not my best handwriting sample, but the other names are written in childish script—including the names of people who are now adults. They must have signed at a much younger age than me.

Finishing with a wobbly letter *t,* I release the pen. Yet another frog lump manifests deep in my esophagus. Why hasn't signing the Family Book stopped the plague?

"One more thing, sweetheart." Holly takes my hand, turns it over, and in a motion too quick to follow, pricks my fingertip with a pin. "Ow!" I protest, but Holly presses my finger—and the bead of blood—to the parchment page of the book.

That explains the brown smudges next to all the names on the family tree.

The crimson bubble of my blood retains its shape for a second before settling into the fibers of the paper, too new and red to match the others.

Signing the Family Book completes a contract with the source of our family magic. That's what Mom told me. *But it's not necessary for you to sign the Book to wield magic. You're a Carrefour, and the magic is yours to master, no matter what.*

Instead of bringing me to Crossroad House when I was young, Mom taught me magic on her own. Together we ran our shop full of gemstones wrought into charms, plus candles, herbs, and other elements of magic. We were lucky to live in a mostly open-minded place; over half the town thought our magical items were solely for fun and tourists, about thirty percent were loyal customers, and only a handful didn't let their kids come to my birthday parties because, you know, "witchcraft." But Mom always said we weren't witches or Wiccans or anything that came with a name...unless that name was Carrefour.

Even though I didn't learn magic on the family estate, I never felt myself lacking, as long as I worked with stones and didn't attempt any other earth elements. Until tonight, that is. When I started spitting up frogs and all sense of earth magic disappeared.

As my blood dries beside my name, the world shifts. My fingertips tingle, waking up, and there's a *pop* inside my middle ear. It's as if some sort of magical plug dissolves, and I can hear the stones I'm wearing on my wrist. The obsidian and turquoise hum their songs of healing and wellness, while the bloodstone croons a promise of protection. *My magic! I haven't forfeited it with my stupidity!*

Equally important: the frog forcing its way up my throat is gone.

"See?" says the woman with the gray hair. "She's looking better already."

"Garnet?" Mom demands, not taking anyone else's word for it.

"I think it's over, Mom."

The people in the room break out in multiple, simultaneous exclamations. I'm too self-conscious for major spell-casting and stone-flattering, but I do raise the bracelets to my face and press them against my cheeks. "Protect me," I whisper.

They don't answer in words, exactly, but I get the impression they want to tell me: *We're trying. We were trying all along.* Warmth floods my limbs.

Lowering my hands, I survey my surroundings. I'm not sure if I should be paying attention to the Carrefour relatives I'm meeting for the first time, or to the house itself, but in the end, the house wins. I know (or can guess) who the people are. Crossroad House has always been a mystery to me.

This room is a library—an honest-to-goodness room dedicated to books, like on the Clue game board. It's got floor-to-ceiling bookshelves, overfed with books standing upright, stacked horizontally, and shoved in diagonally. One wall contains a fireplace flanked by two tall oil paintings. There's also an archway that looks like it should lead to another room, but a curtain is strung over the arch, and bricks peek from behind the fabric. Mom's told me stories about growing up at Crossroad House with her brother and cousins, and there's one that ends in tragedy. I think I know where that opening once led. With a shudder, I reach for the bloodstone amulet again. *Protect me.*

"Garnet is cold," Holly announces to the still-clamoring relatives, misinterpreting my reaction. "Ash, bring your cousin a cup of tea. My chamomile, bay leaf, and lavender blend. In fact, bring a cup for Emerald, too."

She's addressing a boy about my age with strawberry-blond curls and glasses. He nods and scurries from the room.

Then Holly turns to my mother. "You should sit down. You're shaking."

Mom shakes her head. "I sat plenty on the drive." Three hours. One hundred and eighty minutes of frog-filled fun. "We'll take that tea for Garnet to go. I'm not staying in this house a minute more than necessary."

"Emerald." I recognize the woman who steps forward now from the video calls. Windy. Black-haired, golden-skinned, and green-eyed, dressed tonight in a fashionable knee-length sweater, leggings, and boots. "Don't be ridiculous. Of course you have to stay the night. You're exhausted."

"You'll drive straight into a tree," says one of the men. Several people gasp in horror, and he stiffens defensively. "I'm not afraid to say it." This guy has the same strawberry-blond hair as Holly and Ash and large, square glasses that look like something from the eighties. I peg him as Holly's brother, Linden, named after the founder of Crossroad House.

Disclosure: Linden is a popular name in my family. Of the three from the page of the Family Book, two must be present right now. And if you count the figure in the oil painting beside the fireplace—the one with the man wearing an old-fashioned suit and a huge blue gemstone on his ring finger—I suspect all three Lindens are in the room.

Holly holds up her hands. "Can we have everyone who doesn't need to be here leave so Em and I can talk this through?"

Yes, please. This is too many Carrefours at once.

The gray-haired woman departs in a huff, muttering

that she will "update Jasper," and the second man who carried me from the car goes with her. The girl with the spiky black hair follows, typing on her phone as if she has better things to do anyway. Last to go is a teenage boy with skin the color of smoky quartz and tightly curled amber hair, who gently scoops frogs out of the doorway on his way out.

Holly, Windy, and Linden stay behind. Mom scowls at all three of them. "You knew I didn't want to come. You know it's dangerous for Garnet to be here. But you *still* cast a summoning spell. And when my ward blocked the summons, you conjured something else and inflicted it on my daughter!"

"We didn't!" Holly protests with a frustrated stamp of her foot. "What happened to Garnet is not our fault!"

This has gone on long enough. Mom's homecoming is a disaster, she's furious at the wrong people, and it's time for me to confess. With the crowd gone, it seems more possible. I clear my throat, which feels dry and slimy at the same time.

"It's my fault," I croak. "I wanted to come, so I sabotaged your ward, Mom."

Carnelian

Color: *brownish red, from pale orange to almost black*

Magical properties: *smooths new beginnings, calms the temper*

To recharge: *bathe in warm water*

Yup. And I think it's why I lost the use of my magic tonight. The stones stopped singing for me because I deliberately invited in an enemy.

Actions beget consequences.

But in my defense, it wasn't a real enemy. It was family! A family I've never been permitted to know. Mom grew up in a house full of relatives: a brother, cousins, aunts, uncles, grandparents...and I had Mom. Just Mom. And the shadow of everyone who *could* have been part of my life.

My sabotage was simple because Mom's ward had been simply constructed. Most good spells are. She had taken the red candles I fetched from the shop and set them on the kitchen table between two hand mirrors. When she lit the wicks, the flames reflected in the mirrors and in the mirror images inside the mirrors, creating an endless parade of red candles.

Mom focused her gaze on the never-ending flames. "Stand guard against intrusion," she whispered. "Capture it, trap it, never let it go." She tipped her head as if listening to the flame, the candles, or maybe both and then nodded, satisfied. Mom is strongest with stones, but, unlike me, she can sometimes hear other elements.

It was a solid, effective ward. Until she walked away and I nudged one of the mirrors, casting the reflections out of alignment.

"Why?" Mom cries now.

"Because this is your home and your family and you never bring me here!"

"You know why!"

"No, I don't! All I know is there's an augury," I admit, pointing at Windy (which is rude, but whatever). "*She* cast some sort of prophecy before I was born that made you leave and never come back, but you refuse to tell me what it said. Why is this house a danger to me? Is an anvil going to drop on my head, or what?"

Windy, like me and Mom and everyone else in the Carrefour family, wields earth magic. Windy's preferred elements are water and air, just like Mom and I prefer stones. But Windy has an extra gift—divination. Supposedly, when Mom knew she was expecting a baby, she asked Windy to cast an augury, a type of fortune-telling. Whatever prediction Windy conjured made Mom pack her bags and flee the family estate.

So, yeah. When I interfered with Mom's ward, not only was I inviting the summons, I was giving the augury a crack at me. Another reason for my magic to rebound and punish me the way it did. But if *you* had a dire prediction hovering over your head, wouldn't you want to know what it was? Wouldn't you want a chance to fight it?

"No anvils," Windy assures me. "You're perfectly safe inside the house—"

"You don't know that!" Mom snaps.

"Em," says Windy in an exasperated tone. "Have you considered that if you leave the premises Garnet might be afflicted again?"

"What?" The little color left in Mom's face drains away. She drops into a nearby chair. "You would do that to her?"

"No!" Holly slaps her hand on the tabletop, startling her son, Ash, just as he reappears with two mugs of tea. She nods at him, and he puts one in front of me before bringing the other to my mother. "You haven't been listening. We didn't do this to Garnet! The summons Linden and I conjured was an *idée fixe,* as gentle as we could make it, and directed only at you."

I snatch up my mug to wash away the taste of frog and sour stomach. Mom looks at hers longingly, but doesn't drink it. "Then Jasper must have cast it."

Linden shakes his head. "Jasper is sick and weak. Getting worse every day."

Mom's eyes snap up. "We thought that in 1998 and look what happened."

My eyes wander again to the bricked-up archway. I know what happened in 1998 but not what it has to do with Great-Grandfather Jasper being sick.

"My mother was with Jasper for most of the evening," Windy declares. "He didn't have the opportunity to cast a complex spell. Your uncle Flint thinks it's old, deep Carrefour magic, which is why we had the Family Book ready for your arrival. Garnet signed it. Her symptoms ended. It's clear those events are linked."

"What do you mean, *old, deep Carrefour magic*?" Mom's hands tremble as they reach for the mug of Holly's special brew, and I take this as surrender. Holly works with plants the way Mom works with stones and Windy works with air and water. I already feel calmer from drinking the tea, and I bet it's going to put us to sleep fairly quickly.

We're staying the night, at least. A win.

"We don't understand it either," Holly admits. "Flint hasn't been well these past weeks. I'd think he was talking nonsense except he seemed so sharp when we woke him tonight and told him Garnet was in trouble. He made us drag out old books and records and asked Ash to read them to him. Flint remembered some passage he thought might apply to the situation, but we had to comb through a bunch of documents to find it. What was it again?"

Our eyes turn to Ash, and the boy flinches, like someone pinned him in a spotlight. His cheeks flush, and he looks left and right, as if seeking escape, before stammering, "Um…we—we found it in a journal from, like, the 1700s. The handwriting was kinda hard to decipher, and the spelling was weird, but it was about Carrefours being summoned home. Some came willingly and others were forced by pestilence and plague. That was the phrase Flint remembered. *Pestilence and plague.* Flint thought frogs counted as pestilence and said maybe, with Jasper dying, it was *very* important Garnet come home to sign the book."

"But who cast the spell?" I ask.

"No one." Ash blinks at us behind his glasses. "It just…happened."

"Meaning what?" Mom demands. "That the Carrefour magic acted of its own accord? A spell with no one casting it? Has that ever happened before?"

"According to that journal," says Holly, "at least one other time."

I run my fingers over the bloodstone amulet and side-eye the Family Book. I've wanted my name in it ever since I learned it existed. But now that it's done, at the cost of three hours of frog-vomiting, what's my reward?

I glance around the glorious Crossroad House library again and notices that it's...not that glorious. The bookshelves look dusty. The leather chairs near the fireplace are cracked and worn. The ceiling is covered in either mold or damp spots.

"I did warn you she needed to be entered into the book," Linden says to my mother. "I told you that years ago."

Mom scowls. "And I told you to bring the book to me so Garnet could put her blood in the pages."

"Bring it to you? The Family Book never leaves this house!" Linden looks like Mom had suggested he pry up the floorboards and FedEx them to her.

Windy places a gentle hand on Mom's shoulder. "Stay the night. Let us figure this out in the morning, and we'll see if it's safe for Garnet to leave."

"What choice do I have?" Mom asks bitterly. I half expect her to shrug off Windy's comforting hand, but instead she turns to me. "I guess you got what you wanted."

I'm braced for her anger. Ready for it. But what I see in her face isn't anger. It's raw, naked fear, and *that* is a hundred times worse than three hours of frogs.

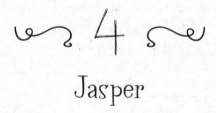

4

Jasper

Color: *many different colors and patterns*

Magical properties: *channels magical energy to stabilize
the body and mind*

To recharge: *bathe in lukewarm running water*

G uilt is a surefire way to make sure someone doesn't enjoy
their win. I clomp glumly up the staircase to the second
floor of Crossroad House behind my mother. Spending the
night here isn't much of a win anyway, since Mom swears
we'll be leaving before breakfast.

Tonight we're borrowing the bedroom of the teenage
boy who delivered the spat-up frogs safely outside. He intro-
duces himself as he leads us upstairs. "I'm Linden, but everyone calls me LJ to not get me confused with my father."

Mom smiles at him, her only smile since we arrived. "I
used to babysit you when you were a toddler."

"I'm sorry I don't remember that, Cousin Emerald," the
boy replies solemnly.

I listen carefully for sarcasm but only detect sincerity.

LJ grabs a few things out of his room and wishes us good night a lot more cheerfully than I would if I was getting kicked out of my space. His room is about the size of mine at home, with one narrow window. The walls are decorated with pictures of athletes and motivational posters with inspirational quotes. The sheets are freshly laundered, although I'm so sleepy I don't care. I feel like I should be hungry, but the obsidian and turquoise, with the help of Holly's tea, have settled my stomach enough that I don't want to disturb it.

Windy drops off clothes for us to borrow. While we change, Mom says, "You are *not* to leave this room tonight."

There's guilt and then there's pride. "I should be allowed to go to the bathroom, Mom. It's like ten feet away."

"To the bathroom, but no farther." Mom sounds exhausted. "Please, Garnet. For once, do what I ask without arguing."

"I don't understand why you won't tell me what Windy's augury said."

"Because," she snaps. "Words. Have. Power."

She means that saying something out loud might invite it to happen. Which sounds like superstition...unless you've just finished barfing up frogs.

⚬✗⚬

Holly's tea puts me down as soon as my head hits the pillow and keeps me in a dreamless sleep for hours. But it's also the reason I need a midnight bathroom visit. Careful not to disturb Mom, I slide out of bed, navigate the unfamiliar room, and open the door.

The wall sconces are not lit, and the single night-light

plugged into an outlet near the floor only amplifies shadows in the hallway. Floorboards groan beneath my weight. Down the hall, a radiator ticks. These are ordinary house noises, and beneath them, in the part of my brain that hears stones sing, I detect other, softer sounds. Wood contracting in the cold. Shutters shivering in the November wind. When LJ escorted us to his room, I didn't have a chance to get an impression of this place other than *old house*. Now, listening to these 125-year-old sighs and murmurs, I'm filled with the sense of a living, breathing entity.

Who cast the spell? I asked.

No one, Ash replied.

He meant no *person*. But what about this house?

Despite the shiver that runs up my back, I shuffle down the hall until I reach the top of the main stairs, where two hallways intersect. The bathroom is straight ahead, the door standing ajar. I take care of business there, and when I come out again, I glance down the staircase, tempted by the opportunity.

There's nothing stopping me from exploring the house other than my promise to Mom. If I'm to be whisked away before breakfast tomorrow, this might be my only chance. When I hesitate, the house's nighttime sounds pause too, as if Crossroad House is holding its breath, watching and waiting to see what I'll do.

Okay. That's it. I've officially creeped myself out. Back to bed and the safety of Mom's company…

"Who are you, then?"

I flinch and freeze at the sound of the voice. A tall, imposing figure emerges from a doorway beyond the bathroom. I relax only when he shuffles forward enough to be seen more clearly in the glow of the nightlight. Yes, *shuffles*—shakily, while leaning on a cane.

"I'm Garnet." I almost add *Your great-granddaughter.* Because there are only two old men in this house and I've been told Uncle Flint is blind, so this has to be Jasper.

Ninety-some years haven't diminished the broadness of his shoulders, although his head hangs low, leading the way as his body follows. He's dressed in a flannel robe, belted at the waist, with pajama bottoms showing below the hem and his feet stuffed into leather moccasins. The ivory skin on his face is tight over the cheekbones but hangs loosely beneath his jaw. Sparse gray hair contrasts with bushy, untamed eyebrows. Planting his cane solidly on the floor, he leans on it and eyes me up and down. "You don't look like Emerald," he says, which means he knows who I am.

And no, I don't look like my mother. People have said that my whole life, and most of them expect an explanation.

Mom is petite and blond and burns in the sun if she isn't covered head to toe in sunscreen. Meanwhile, at twelve, I'm already as tall as she is, with an olive complexion and thick, dark hair that tends to break combs. I open my mouth to give my usual response, but Great-Grandfather Jasper beats me to it. "You take after your father."

My mouth drops open. "Did you know him?"

"I met him," Jasper admits, as if the meeting was brief and he didn't approve.

This is an unexpected gift. My father is "uninvolved." That's a common term used at school by classmates with single parents. But most of my peers with an "uninvolved" parent at least know their name, have a few old pictures, and sometimes get impersonal birthday cards and awkward Christmas presents.

I have nothing. No name. Not a single photograph. Just the vague explanation that my father was an archaeology student who briefly dated my mother before going off to travel the world. My image of him is shaped by what I see in the mirror.

Before I can ask more, Jasper takes a step forward, and his ankle turns in the soft moccasins. Weakly, he stabs the floor with his cane, trying to regain stability.

"Do you need help?" I rush forward, slipping under his non-cane-wielding arm. "I can wake someone."

"No need. You're a sturdy girl. You'll do just fine."

His arm tightens around my shoulder. I try to turn us around, to direct him back to his room, but a buzzing rises in my ears, and my own balance shifts. The hallway turns over, the night-light sliding up the wall. My feet stumble over each other, and suddenly it's me clutching Jasper for support instead of the other way around.

"Easy, child," he says. "This way."

The hallway wavers, and the bloodstone amulet on my wrist wails. I thought I was taking him back to his room, but now LJ's room is in front of us. My eyesight dims to a small gray band, and I stagger forward to seize the doorknob.

"Sleep," says Jasper, releasing me. "You'll feel better in the morning."

I hang on to the door, not trusting my legs to hold my weight. I need a moment's rest before trying to make it back to bed without falling.

While I cling to the door, Great-Grandfather Jasper walks away with a steady tread, no need for his cane at all.

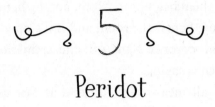

5

Peridot

Color: *olive green*

Magical properties: *reveals the true nature of places and people*

To recharge: *place in sunlight*

R aised voices. Footsteps in the hall. Doors opening and closing.

These are the sounds that wake me in the morning. Sunlight streams through the narrow window, and Mom's side of the bed is empty, the covers thrown back and not replaced neatly the way she does at home.

I sit up slowly, remembering the sudden attack of dizziness from last night. I barely managed to get back into bed. Dropping my bare feet to the floor, I test my balance and strength and find nothing wrong.

You'll feel better in the morning, Jasper said. He's right. Either he somehow guessed what was wrong with me—or he knew for a fact. *Mom suspected him of inflicting the frogs on me no matter what her cousins said. Maybe she was right.*

My attention is wrenched back to the voices in the hall-way. One of them belongs to Mom, and by her tone, something is wrong. I cross the room and crack open the door.

"After the coroner signs off, the cremation can take place," Linden is saying.

"Oh, by all means, let's do this as fast as possible," Mom snaps sarcastically. "Unless you want to wait and see who else dies. Maybe we can get a group discount."

"Shhh!" Linden glances around. "Watch what you say."

"Why? Because the house is listening?"

My mouth drops open. Did Mom just say the crazy thing I was thinking last night? Even more surprising is Linden's answer: "If you want to put it that way."

"So you expect me to shut up until Jasper names you as his heir."

Linden adjusts his clunky glasses. "That would be helpful."

In mundane families, property is usually passed down from father to child. But control of the Carrefour magic isn't property, and it doesn't work like that. Carrefour heirs are handpicked by their predecessor. Everyone except Windy thinks Jasper is planning to pick Linden, his grandnephew—but what if he died before he chose anyone?

"Aren't you and Garnet leaving anyway?" Linden looks at me through the crack in the doorway as if he knew I was there all along.

Mom, however, is startled to see me. She pushes the door open and crowds me back inside by entering herself. "You will not rush this," she says to Linden over her shoulder. "He deserves a service and a burial. Cremating him would be wildly inappropriate."

She closes the door between them, and, with guilt in my stomach like a shard of glass, I ask, "Did Great-Grandfather Jasper die?" *I should have called for help last night!*

Except at the end, he seemed in better shape than I did.

"No," Mom says. "Uncle Flint did."

"Uncle Flint?" I blink at her. "The one who searched a bunch of family records to figure out what was happening to me? Or, I mean, got Ash to do it?"

"Yes." Mom smooths the hair away from my face, sadness written clearly on her own. "He was our historian right to the end. But he was very sick, Garnet. And old."

Not as old as his father, Jasper, but definitely in his seventies. Here's what I know about Uncle Flint: Never married. No children. And on the fateful day in 1998 when a wing of Crossroad House caught fire, Flint ran into the flames to rescue his sister, Opal.

My grandmother.

Not only did he fail to reach her, he was injured in the attempt, blinded, and left in precarious health for the rest of his life.

Mom takes me by the shoulders. "I don't like Linden's plans, so I need to stay to make sure Uncle Flint is given the respect he's due. Not in this house. We can get a room at a hotel in the next town over. But I'm afraid this means we can't go home today."

"I don't *want* to go home." For what? School? I don't care if I miss a few days. And I'm sorry Mom's uncle died, but if it delays our departure, even a little...

"We'll be here until lunchtime, at least. Unless I drive you to the hotel now and come back alone..." Her gaze grows unfocused as she plays out that scenario in her head.

"Please don't leave me in a hotel!" I beg. "Can't I get a tour of the house? Or a chance to meet my cousins?"

"I guess it would be all right if Ash shows you around the house. Maybe LJ can look after you. Or River." That must be the teenage girl with the spiky hair and nose ring. It would be embarrassing to be babysat by her—or LJ—but it's better than being stashed in a hotel.

"Stay here," Mom says finally. "Let me talk to Holly."

After she leaves, I change into my own jeans. My healing and protection stones have no voice left this morning, their magic depleted. I take the bracelets off and whisper my thanks to each and every stone before placing them on the windowsill to recharge in sunlight.

Then I wait. Just when I've started to wonder if Mom decided I should stay confined to this room, someone knocks. "Come in!"

The door opens, and Ash sticks his curly head around the corner. "Um, hi. It's me. Ash. Your cousin."

"Yeah, we met." We weren't introduced and we hardly spoke, but he did hand me a cup of tea.

He pushes the door open farther. "Your mom asked me to show you around the house. If you're interested."

I jump up from my seat on the bed. "Yes. Please." *Get me out of this room!*

He offers me a silvery packet. "Do you want Pop-Tarts? It doesn't look like anybody's cooking breakfast today, so I brought you these. They're not toasted...."

I don't care. Grabbing the packet out of his hand, I rip it open and shove a corner of Frosted Strawberry into my mouth. "I'm starving!" I garble around a mouthful of stiff pastry.

Ash looks taken aback by my enthusiasm. "We can wait till you finish."

I shake my head and make a shooing motion with my free hand. "I can walk and chew at the same time."

Ash leads me into the hallway, where he shoves his hands in his pockets and starts reciting like a tour guide. "You're in LJ's room, and River is next door. Across the hall is Uncle Linden and Aunt—uh, actually it's only Uncle Linden now, but never mind that—and next to him is Flint. *Was* Flint."

I glance uneasily at the closed door. Is his body still in there?

"He was cool," Ash says. "I used to read to him. Since, you know, he couldn't."

"That was nice of you."

"I wasn't the only one." Ash points to the closed door beyond the bathroom. "That's Jasper's room."

I know. A mouthful of Pop-Tart prevents me saying it aloud, but I shiver, remembering my middle-of-the-night encounter.

"Down there—" Ash points down the hallway perpendicular to this one. "Windy and her mom." Then he makes a face. "You probably don't care where everyone sleeps."

"It's helpful." Though not particularly interesting. It occurs to me that Ash doesn't want to do this, that he's only taking me around because his mom is making him.

That stings my pride. Maybe I should tell him he needn't bother…except that if Mom is determined to take me away, this might be my only chance to tour Crossroad House.

So when Ash takes the stairs down to the first floor, I follow.

Sunlight from the window over the front door illuminates the stairwell, catching the peeling edge of wallpaper in the corner and cobwebs adorned with the corpses of dead bugs. Details I didn't notice on my way upstairs last night. "Down here," Ash says as we reach the bottom, "we've got the parlor on our left, and the library to the—"

"No! Don't come here!"

Ash freezes. In the hallway, a woman is speaking into a phone—an old rotary phone that sits on a table and is attached to the wall by a cord. "I know you don't understand, but you *can't* come here!"

The woman has shoulder-length hair the kind of bright burgundy that comes out of a box, ironed poker-straight. I don't remember seeing her in the library last night, and I think I would have, with hair that color. When she spots us on the stairs, she scowls with a thousand-watt laser-beam glare, then turns her back and starts whispering harshly into the phone.

Cheeks flushed, Ash beckons me down the hallway that bisects the first floor. "That's my aunt Rose," he whispers. "She's not happy about being here."

No kidding. "Did she get summoned too?"

"When she heard they were doing that to your mom, she came voluntarily." After delivering that bit of family gossip, he returns to his tour. "The sitting room is on the right, and over there's the dining room."

Peeking into each dark room, I get an impression of heavy curtains closed against the world. The carpet runner in the hallway is worn, and the lights are dim in their dirty glass covers. Last night, Crossroad House gave off the sense of a watchful entity—mysterious and sinister. Now, it feels like the house is cringing in embarrassment, all its dirty secrets laid bare in the daytime.

Ash keeps going. "That's the TV room. We've got streaming, but it goes down three or four times a week. Good luck making your phone work. We're in a dead zone."

Of course this is a dead zone.

We reach the end of the hallway, where there are three doors. On one side is a pair of sliding glass doors opening to a covered porch.

"The kitchen is here." Ash leads me into a spacious room on the other side, but we stop at the sight of three unhappy people sitting at the table. In the middle is the steely-haired woman who opened the door to Crossroad House last night, now weeping into a tissue. Windy sits on one side, comforting her, and the spiky-haired teenager sits on the other side. Hastily, Ash and I back out into the hallway again.

The Pop-Tarts form a lump in my stomach. I had, for a couple of minutes, forgotten about the death in the house.

Ash grimaces apologetically. "Tempest and Flint were the last of their generation. Now she's the only one left, so this is extra upsetting for her."

"Tempest is Windy's mother? And the girl is Windy's daughter?"

"River." Ash looks surprised I don't know this already.

I laugh. Falsely and embarrassedly. "Guess I should study the Family Book."

"The names are a clue," Ash explains. "Because everybody's name matches—"

"—the earth element they channel," I finish. I do know *some* family traditions.

Windy's branch of the family works in wind and water magic.

My mother's line, up and down the family tree, are named after gems and stones.

Ash's branch has plant names.

There used to be Carrefours who harnessed their magic with fire, but Mom says that branch died out before she was born.

Ash reverts to tour guide mode, indicating the third door. "This leads to my family's wing. It was built as servant quarters in the eighteen hundreds, but my grandparents renovated it in the seventies. Do you want to head over? We've got an Xbox. We'll have to let my little brother Oak play with us, though."

"Okay, but..." *Dare I ask?* "Can I see the pool first?"

Ash blinks at me from behind his smudgy glasses. "The pool?"

November in New England is not swimming season, but the pool is in the one photo Mom saved from Crossroad House. *Every day of the summer, we'd hang out by the pool. Windy had a parade of boyfriends, and it never rained if she didn't want it to.* It was in most of the stories she told me of her teenage years.

"Okaaaay." Ash shrugs. I reach for the sliding glass door, but he exclaims, "Not that way! The porch isn't safe to walk on." He beckons me down the hall, through the sitting room to a sun room with windows on three sides and a door to the lawn. When we step through it, I see why Ash didn't want to exit through the porch. The roof over the porch sags in the middle. Crossroad House is literally falling apart.

An overgrown path leads away from the house. A few steps from the deathtrap porch, we pass a stone-lined hole in the ground. "That used to be a goldfish pond," Ash says. "Now it's where Oak throws his broken toys."

My heart sinks by the time we reach the point where the dry, brown lawn drops off into a sunken area. The swimming pool is an empty cement pit. Its walls are green with mold, and the bottom is filled with mud. "Mom says it used to be nice," Ash remarks.

I'm so disappointed, I can't speak.

"Let's walk around to the front of the house," my tour guide suggests. "I bet you didn't get a good look last night."

Nope. I was vomiting frogs and carried in like a baby.

At the top of the driveway, a stone wall ornaments the base of the house. It's crumbling, like everything else here. Concrete steps cut through the wall, leading to a front door and two huge windows. Five normal-sized windows span the second floor, with three gabled ones on the third floor. Ash has started talking about the "retaining wall" when something around the corner catches my eye. Leaving Ash behind, I walk along the width of the house until I can fully see the other side.

It's the remnants of another wing. Nothing is left but the foundation and fragments of blackened framework. This is the wing that burned down in 1998, and these ghostly studs and joists are a gut-wrenching reminder of the fire, the woman who died in it, and the people who were damaged by it.

By the time Ash catches up with me, my body has gone cold. I reach instinctively for my bloodstone amulet, forgetting that I left it recharging on a windowsill. "Why wasn't this torn down years ago?"

Ash hunches his shoulders. "The house doesn't want it torn down."

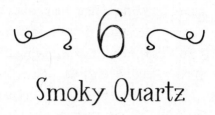

Smoky Quartz

Color: *tinted brown or dark gray*

Magical properties: *addresses issues of property and unfinished business*

To recharge: *wrap tightly in cloth, put away in a dark place*

"The *house* doesn't want it torn down?" I gape at Crossroad House, trying not to see the windows as eyes.

"Uh, let's talk over here." Ash leads me away from the house, toward a bench outside a freestanding structure that seems to be serving as a garage for a lawn mower, a tractor, and a couple of cars.

Like he doesn't want Crossroad House to eavesdrop.

Ash plops himself on the bench. "I can't believe your mom hasn't explained this."

"You mean, explained that the house is alive?" I sink down beside him. My knees shake, and I grip them with both hands, to stop them from running away and taking me with them.

"It's not alive. It's an embodiment of the family magic.

And Jasper. That's why the house is in the condition it is. We *think,* if Jasper dies and a new heir takes over, everything will get better." He sighs. "If I was in charge, the first thing I'd do is pull down that burned wing and put in a garden."

He turns to me as if something has occurred to him. "Can you do magic?"

"Yes!" I glare at him. "Why wouldn't I?"

He looks embarrassed. "We were speculating before you got here. If you could develop magic growing up so far from Crossroad House."

"My mother trained me," I tell him indignantly. "I listen to stones and coax power out of them. It's the same thing you do with herbs." He looks at me funny. "My mom said that Holly's specialty is medicinal herbs, so I assumed—"

"I'm not the same as my mom," Ash says. "Mom and Aunt Rose make medicines and teas. I'm more like Uncle Linden and LJ. Except, not as powerful. I'll show you."

Ash stands and heads for a sad dandelion that looks like the autumn weather is inches from doing it in. Squatting, he cups his hand around the bud. He whispers to it, and the bud swells, golden petals unfolding until the flower reaches its cheerful sunshine-y peak.

"That's amazing!"

"It's just a dandelion." Ash brushes his hands on his jeans.

"But you can do it with other plants, right?"

"Still makes me a gardener."

"If you ask me, this place could use a gardener."

Ash snorts a laugh but looks glum. "Uncle Linden and

LJ can work with trees. Last winter, we had a problem with flooding eroding the foundation under the front steps. Windy and River diverted the path of the water, and the Lindens made trees shift their roots so it would stay that way. Me, I'm the Flower Guy, which is pretty depressing when everything I plant at Crossroad House wilts and dies." He nods his head toward the already-fading dandelion.

The crunch of tires on gravel draws our attention. Two vehicles, a hearse and a small blue car, pull in at the top of the driveway. Men get out of the hearse and remove a stretcher. A Black woman with mahogany skin and short brown corkscrew hair gets out of the car.

Mom and Linden appear at the front door of Crossroad House. The men climb the steps to speak with Mom. Linden passes them and approaches the woman from the blue car.

"That's Aunt Victoria," says Ash. "She and Uncle Linden got divorced."

Linden takes his ex-wife into his arms and kisses her. Not a peck on the cheek. He *kisses her* kisses her.

"They don't look divorced!" I want to avert my eyes, but the smooching ends, and they enter the house, hand in hand.

"They only did it so she won't be part of the family during the transition. They'll get back together after Jasper dies. If he dies."

"What?" I don't think that fully conveys my confusion, so I repeat it. *"What?"*

"Every time there's a transfer of power, people die here. Do you know what happened the last time Jasper was 'dying'?" Ash gives the word air quotes.

I glance at the burned wing. "That wouldn't have been in 1998, would it?"

"Right. Jasper had an inoperable brain tumor. Doctors gave him six months to live. During that time, four family members died, two were injured, and a girl disappeared. By the end of the six months, Jasper's tumor was gone. The doctors said it was a miracle, but it wasn't. It was Carrefour magic."

I feel queasy. Mom's hints and vague answers...why didn't she tell me the rest of this outright? "I thought three people died the day of the fire. I didn't know about a fourth. Or a missing girl." Grandmother Opal died in the fire, but she wasn't the only casualty I knew of. The family couldn't call the fire department because the phone line was down. So my grandmother's cousin and her husband—Linden, Holly, and Rose's parents—jumped into a car and drove to town as fast as they could. Too fast. The car went off the road and hit a telephone pole, killing them both.

"Windy's father got pneumonia and died about a month after the fire," Ash says. "My mom says no one understood what was happening at the time, but when Jasper miraculously recovered, they figured it out in hindsight. And it reminded them of the stories about people dying around the time the *last* heir passed, when Jasper took over. So you see why everyone is nervous about this transition. Whether Jasper recovers or passes on...things could get dangerous."

My fingers seek the absent bloodstone amulet again, and I wish I had *some* kind of stone on me, for comfort if nothing else. "Last night I met Jasper in the hall outside the bathroom. He leaned on my shoulder...and I got really dizzy."

Ash examines the ground for several seconds. When he lifts his face, his cheeks are aflame. "He stole from your life energy. Took some of your strength for himself."

My windpipe squeezes my breath into a tiny whisper. "That's not possible."

"It is." Ash stares at me grimly. "He's fighting death. I think—no, I *know* Uncle Linden willingly gives him small doses. I hope LJ doesn't, but I'm not sure. And those are just the volunteers." He takes off his glasses and cleans them with the hem of his shirt. "The most vulnerable are the weak, like your great-uncle Flint, and the old, like Windy's mother. And the clueless. Sorry."

I gulp. Mom never prepared me for magic like this.

"Also the spouses," Ash continues. "Sometimes family members are spared and we lose spouses instead. That's why Uncle Linden divorced his wife and made her go live in town. It's why Aunt Rose left her fiancé to come here. It's why Windy never married River's dad and why—" He cuts himself off, and his eyes dart away from me.

But I can guess what he was going to say. *Why you don't know your father.*

"What about your dad?" I ask. "He was one of the men who carried me into the house last night, right?"

Ash nods. "My dad's been taking care of this house a long time. He's the reason more of it hasn't fallen down. Dad thinks he's earned some loyalty."

Whose loyalty? Jasper's? The house's? I've been talking to stones my whole life—it isn't crazy to think a house has feelings too. "Why do other people die or disappear when the family heir is near death?"

"We're not sure, and there aren't many families like us left in the world to consult. Maybe earth magic automatically tries to preserve the existing heir. Maybe transitioning power from one heir to the next burns up a certain amount of life energy. But a lot of people in the family think it happens when the heir doesn't give up and go quietly. It's very likely 1998 should have been a transition year, but Jasper resisted."

Now I get it. Why Mom wants me away from here.

"The girl who disappeared," I begin. "Who was—"

"Garnet!"

LJ strides toward us, a broad smile lighting his face. My own expression sours. This is exactly the wrong moment to interrupt Ash's "house tour," now that he's spilling all the beans.

But LJ hasn't come to babysit. "May I escort you back to the house?" he asks politely. "Jasper would like to speak with you."

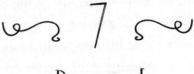

Diamond

Color: *colorless*

Magical properties: *enhances power and energy,*
both positive and negative

To recharge: *diamonds need to be cleaned, not charged*

LJ leads the way, looking as cheerful as a Boy Scout earning a badge. "Jasper can be stern," he warns me, apparently not realizing I've already met the man. "It's the way he is. He doesn't mean anything by it."

I'm more worried about him being a life-energy-sucking vampire than his sternness. Thanks to Ash, I'm no longer clueless. I won't let Jasper near me. He's ninety-three years old. How fast can he move?

Ash marches beside me, fists clenched.

LJ ushers us into the library. I recognize the chair I was propped up in and the desk where Holly made me sign the Family Book. Now, with a clear head, I pay attention to the details I missed. The lectern that holds the Family Book in a place of honor. The figures in the life-sized paintings that flank the fireplace. I already identified Old Linden—the Linden born in 1874—seated in a wing-backed leather chair and prominently displaying a blue-toned gemstone ring. Today I notice that his family flanks him in the dark background of the painting as if they're of lesser importance: two small children and a wife holding an infant draped in yards of cloth.

The second painting centers on an attractive woman with intelligent gray eyes. Her bronze-colored hair is worn in a style from the 1940s, and she's seated in Old Linden's chair surrounded by four children—two nearly grown young men, a boy about ten years old, and a little girl barely old enough to stand. The second-oldest boy has a startling pair of bushy eyebrows, which makes me think he must be a young Jasper.

Jasper himself is waiting in a chair that looks like the chair from the paintings. It's a lot worse for wear, the leather cracked and torn. Jasper, however, looks stronger than he did yesterday. His hand is steady when he waves me forward. "Garnet, it's good to see you looking well today."

I cross my arms and glare. "No thanks to you."

He looks past me. "Thank you for bringing her, LJ. You and Ash can go."

LJ nods briskly, but Ash stares at the floor and mumbles, "I'm staying."

Jasper's hairy eyebrows twitch, and LJ makes a discreet, urgent gesture beckoning Ash to the door. As for me, I'm startled by Ash's declaration. I expected him to bolt as fast as he could. Instead, he casts me a glance and whispers, "It's not right. You don't know how things work here."

Turning back to Jasper, I declare, "I want him to stay. If he can't, then I won't either."

Jasper barks out a laugh. "Ash may stay. I wasn't planning to interrogate you with rubber hoses and bamboo under the fingernails, but if you feel safer with him here..." He gestures dismissively at LJ, who leaves the room and closes the door behind him.

Rubber hoses and bamboo under the fingernails. Does he think that's funny? I don't bother to hide my fury.

"You're feisty," he says, his eyes alight. "Just like your mother. I'm curious what you know about our family. Has Emerald left you completely ignorant?"

I'm not in the mood for a quiz, but Mom did *not* leave me ignorant, and I won't let him think she did. "The name Carrefour is French for 'crossroad,' and Crossroad House is built on an important intersection of ley lines."

Jasper's hairy eyebrows waggle. "What, in your understanding, are ley lines?"

I grit my teeth. "Ley lines are veins of earth magic crossing the globe. Every historical structure of great importance was built on a ley line—pyramids, temples, even the US Capitol. Where ley lines intersect, they're especially powerful. Crossroad House is built on one of those places."

"No." Jasper looks pleased to catch me in an error, although I don't think I made one. "The *original* Crossroad House was built on the intersection of ley lines."

This is news to me, but when I look at Ash, he nods. "Old House. It's nothing but ruins now."

Jasper continues his test. "What do you know about family-linked earth magic?"

"There used to be many families like ours. Some were famous, like the Borgias and the Medicis. Most are gone now, or they don't acknowledge their magic."

"Yes. The Old Crossroad House was built by Diamon Carrefour in 1730. He was a castoff from one of the European families—a renegade son who changed his name on arrival in the Americas." Jasper leans forward, placing his arms across his knees. "Do you know what rituals are needed to establish a family's link to earth magic based on ley lines?"

Here I falter. "No, I don't."

"No surprise there. I doubt Emerald ever understood. First, you must harness the energy of the ley lines by building on them. Secondly, you must live and raise children there. If family members move away and don't bring their children back, the power of the entire family is diminished."

I'd love to ask if the real first step for harnessing Carrefour magic began with appropriating the land from indigenous people. Instead, I recap his point. "You're saying, by raising me somewhere else, Mom weakened the family magic."

"To an extent. It first happened in the eighteen hundreds when adult Carrefour children moved away from the family home and the heir at the time gambled away a fortune. The original house was lost to bankruptcy and sold to another family. Luckily, Linden Carrefour"—Jasper indicates the painting—"was able to buy the property back in 1892 after the new owners were murdered by their servants—"

"Supposedly," Ash mutters.

"—and the house was burned to the ground."

"Conveniently," Ash adds under his breath.

"Linden built the second Crossroad House slightly removed from the intersection of ley lines. He reestablished the Carrefour line and re-amassed the family fortune."

Why *slightly removed*? Earth magic would be strongest where the ley lines intersect, so why not clear the ruins and build the new house on the same spot? Before I can ask, Jasper's smoldering gaze settles on Ash. "There was nothing convenient about the loss of Old House. It was a devastating setback to start over again, and you would not live as comfortably as you do now if not for the effort and magic your ancestor poured into the current house."

I bet Old Linden got the land for cheap after murders and fire. I almost say so, but the wall sconces flicker and dim right then, like Crossroad House is offended by my cousin's irreverent remarks. Ash eyes the light fixtures uneasily, his cheeks flushing. I change the subject. "You've got the original Linden's ring, but you let it get dirty and gross. Are you a stone worker or not?"

Jasper is wearing the same ring as Old Linden. In the painting, it's clean and exquisitely rendered, the flat table-cut gem an icy blue. The setting is gold, the band carved enamel. But the ring on Jasper's finger is grimy, the band so tarnished it's unrecognizable. The gemstone's grumbling has been building since I entered this room, growing from a barely audible hum to a hard-to-ignore throbbing.

The lights return to normal as Jasper chuckles at my criticism and looks at the ring on his hand. "You're right. This ring deserves better treatment. What can you tell me about it?"

Another test. But this one I'll pass. "Three and a half carats. A table-cut blue diamond." I take a few steps closer, attracted by the gem's voice. "And powerful."

The door to the library bursts open with such force that it hits the wall and swings back. Mom strides into the room, blond hair flying behind her like a warrior goddess. Her blazing eyes are fixed on her grandfather. "I told you to stay away from my daughter!"

I back away from him, annoyed that I let the ring distract me.

Jasper's reply is calm in the face of her fury. "And I told you that I need to become acquainted with her before I choose an heir."

"You've already chosen, and everyone knows it."

"Almost thirteen years you've been gone, Emerald. Don't presume to know what I have or have not decided."

Mom lifts her chin. "The funeral director says we can have a service for Uncle Flint and burial here tomorrow."

Jasper shakes his head. "Linden and I discussed cremation as a simpler option."

"I will not allow you to end his existence on this earth with fire." Her voice is a thunderclap in the room.

A taut silence follows as my mother and her grandfather face off. Jasper breaks the impasse. "Very well. I leave it to you to make the arrangements. It is good to have you back, Emerald. We have missed your...forceful personality."

I can't tell if he's joking. He turns back to me. "I'll find you again later. I must commit myself to the task no father should have to do: writing a eulogy for my son."

We are dismissed. Ash doesn't need to be told twice.

He's out the door like a bullet. Mom takes me by the hand and we follow with a little more dignity. But as soon as she shuts the library door between us and him, Mom whirls around and hugs me. "Baby, you need to stay away from him."

"I know. Ash explained it to me." I pull away and look her in the eyes.

Mom knows me well enough to hear the unspoken accusation. "I hoped I'd never *have* to explain these things to you." She addresses Ash. "Thank you."

"No problem," he says, scuffing his shoe against the threadbare hallway rug.

"I'm sorry, Garnet." She sighs heavily. "I'll explain everything. It's time you learned. But first, I want you to meet my brother."

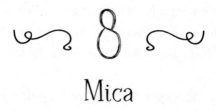

Mica

Color: *multiple colors, including pink to violet, gray to black*

Magical properties: *natural shield against anger,
spite, and violence*

To recharge: *rub briskly with a dry cloth*

There's no reason to be nervous. But I've never met a hermit before, let alone one who doesn't speak.

The spiral wooden steps that lead to the attic are behind a door near Jasper's bedroom. Uncle Mica hasn't left the third floor of Crossroad House in years, according to Mom. Considering the state of the rest of the place, I expect cobwebs with huge spiders and dressmaker dummies covered in sheets posed in corners to frighten visitors.

Instead, the stairwell gets brighter as we go. When I reach the top, I step onto the floor of the attic, which is illuminated by a huge—and surprisingly clean—picture window. Light bounces around the open space, breaking into twirling prisms, dancing spots, and brilliant colors.

My ears pick up a pleasant hum and I see that the

attic is filled with happy, singing gemstones. Sun-catchers strung with crystals hang from the rafters. Baskets and bins filled with colorful polished stones line several sets of shelves.

Across the room, a man seated on a stool in front of a workbench swivels to face me. He doesn't have wild hair or the bushy beard I've been imagining. His hair is short and neatly combed, a darker blond than Mom's. The slow smile that broadens at the sight of me overshadows the burn scars on the left side of his face.

During the fire in 1998, eighteen-year-old Mica dragged his unconscious uncle, Flint, out of the ground floor of the burning wing. Despite his own injuries, he tried to go back inside to save his mother, who was trapped on the second floor. Linden was forced to tackle and restrain him, or we might have lost him, too. That's what my mom told me.

According to doctors, Mica's scars did not prevent him from speaking. But some injuries run too deep to be visible.

So today, when Mom says, "Mica, meet your niece, Garnet," he doesn't call out a welcome.

I've never been fond of huggy adults, but something makes me walk straight toward this man and throw my arms around his neck. He stiffens, but only for a moment. Then he melts into my hug and pats my back. When I step backward, he grins and wipes tears from his eyes.

Mom hugs him next, and when they let go, they give each other rambunctious little shoves, like children. "I rescued Garnet from Jasper just now," Mom says.

Uncle Mica's grin turns into a scowl.

"He was quizzing me on family history and the blue

diamond he wears," I tell them. "And the old house. Where is that, exactly?"

Uncle Mica motions for me to follow him to the picture window. It overlooks the empty swimming pool and, beyond that, a cemetery. Farther away, in a patch of woods, two stone columns stand like lonely soldiers guarding a lost treasure. Half hidden among the bare-branched trees, I glimpse a pile of stone and brick. My uncle taps me on the shoulder, then shakes his head and his finger, back and forth.

"You're forbidden to go anywhere near that place," Mom says, in case I don't grasp his meaning.

She's making that tight expression she always has whenever she says it's not safe for me at Crossroad House, and I remember what Windy said on the night I arrived: *You're perfectly safe* inside *the house*. "Does this have to do with the augury?" I ask.

"It does," she admits. "And I *will* explain it to you, but Windy has offered to come to our hotel tonight and cast a new one. I want to see if it's changed before I give you details. I can tell you that several people have disappeared from the grounds of Old House over the last century. Uncle Flint seemed to think the place consumes life energy."

Like Jasper does, apparently. "Ash said there was a girl who disappeared from here the summer of the 1998 fire."

Mom nods. "She was staying over with us for a couple of days. She took a walk around the ruins, and no one ever saw her again."

Uncle Mica frowns suddenly and picks up a bottle of Windex from the floor. He sprays the window and wipes away a greasy film with a paper towel, which he then drops into a wastebasket already filled to the brim. This glass might be the cleanest thing in Crossroad House, but only because my uncle is fighting to keep it that way.

"I told you I'd answer your questions," Mom says. "So ask away."

"Ash told me Jasper can steal life energy. Is that true?"

Uncle Mica nods, and Mom says, "Yes. His position as the Carrefour heir gives him a certain power over the other members of the family. The earth magic of the crossroad flows through him to us. He can cut it off, and he can take other things from us as well. I know this must sound scary...."

I assume she sees the horror on my face, but she doesn't know the reason for it. She thinks I'm shocked by what Jasper can do, but what really strikes me is even worse: When Jasper left me clinging to the doorknob last night, did he return to his own room? Or did he pay a visit to his son's room first? They said Flint was sick, but was he really on the verge of death if he was well enough to make Ash and Holly search through books on my behalf?

"Garnet? You've gone pale. Do you need to sit down?" Mom takes me by the elbow, while Uncle Mica grabs his stool and wheels it in my direction.

"No! I'm okay." I pull my arm away from Mom and ignore the stool—but I do brace one hand on the wall. "Ash also told me that when Jasper was sick before, other people died and he got better. And you said something to Linden this morning about a group discount with the funeral home. That wasn't a joke, was it?"

"I shouldn't have said that," Mom admits ruefully. "Words have power. I was angry with Linden for planning a cremation, of all things. But yes, Jasper had cancer that was supposed to be terminal. Every time someone died that year, and when that girl disappeared, he got better instead of worse. *That* is why I didn't want to come here, Garnet."

She's still mad about my sabotage. Having seen the decrepit state of the house and grounds—and after meeting Jasper—I should agree with Mom that this is a place to avoid at all costs. But I can't.

"Then I wouldn't have seen Uncle Mica's workshop!" I protest. "This is the most beautiful place in Crossroad House. It was worth coming to see this alone!" Stones and crystals around the room sing out wordlessly in joy and agreement. (I told you they like to be flattered.) Uncle Mica grins and nudges his sister.

Mom exhales in exasperation and checks the time on her phone. "Have a look around. Then we need to check in at the hotel."

Uncle Mica gives me a tour of his workshop, explaining his work rather eloquently without words. I've seen Uncle Mica's finished work before. Almost every "charmed" item we sell in our shop comes from him. But seeing the jewelry-making in progress is fascinating. Clearly he makes amulets and talismans for more than just Mom to sell.

"He has an Etsy shop," Mom explains when I mention this.

"You do?" My uncle grins and makes an *E* and a *B* with his fingers. "And you're on eBay?" Uncle Mica is not the kind of hermit I've seen in movies.

In addition to the workshop, the third floor contains a tiny apartment where Uncle Mica lives. There's also a large room toward the front of the house that looks the way I expected the attic to look—dusty and full of boxes and discarded household items. It isn't dark, though. Three gabled windows recently Windexed by Uncle Mica illuminate faded wallpaper.

"That's the old nursery," Mom says.

"Nursery?" I repeat, appalled. "Who would put a baby in the attic?"

"That's what people used to do, Garnet. They stuck their kids on the third floor, out of sight and out of hearing, and hired governesses to look after them." Mom shudders dramatically. "The habit went out of fashion long before Mica and I were born."

"Lucky for you." I firmly close the door to that room. "Poor kids."

Mom gives Uncle Mica a hug. "I've missed you so much."

He signals one-handedly. *Me too.*

"We'll be back for the funeral," Mom says. "But it's time I get Garnet away from this house."

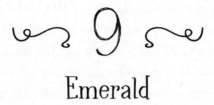

Emerald

Color: *yellow-green to blue-green*

Magical properties: *helps in navigating relationships,*
wards against enchantment

To recharge: *run water over the stone regularly*

We descend from the attic to find Ash's dad searching for us on the second floor. He's a tall, lanky man with a receding hairline, and, today at least, a little disheveled. "Holly needs to talk to you!" he exclaims as soon as he sees us. "Before you try to leave."

"Try to leave?" Mom repeats. Her tone says *Try and stop me.*

"Yes," he says firmly. "You need to see what happened to Holly." The distress in his voice shuts down any argument from Mom. He leads us downstairs and through the house to the wing where his family lives.

In a kitchen much smaller than the one in the main house, Holly is sitting at a table, and her sister, Rose, is mashing something up with a mortar and pestle. Mom and

I gasp when we get a good look at Holly. She immediately says, "It's better than it was."

Angry red blotches cover her face, her arms, and—if her scratching is any clue—pretty much the rest of her. A little boy with hair like dandelion fluff stands beside her, trying to smear white paste from a tube on the spots. "Hold still, Mommy."

"It's okay, Oak." She kisses him on the side of the head. "I don't think hydrocortisone cream is going to work."

Rose shows Oak a greenish paste inside her stone mortar. "Magical ailments need magical remedies. Help me put this on her."

"What happened?" Mom demands.

"Simon and I were on our way to the grocery store," Holly explains, while Rose and Oak finger-paint the green gook on her cheeks and arms. "We hadn't gotten far before I started feeling uneasy. Then the hives began. The farther down the dirt lane we drove, the more of them broke out."

"I didn't know what to do." Ash's dad paces the room. "They kept popping up like she was being stung by invisible bees. I didn't know whether to call 911 or drive her straight to the hospital!"

Holly clears her throat warningly, tipping her head toward Oak. Her husband stops pacing and makes an obvious effort to appear calmer, giving his wide-eyed son a smile. "I knew right away," Holly continues the story. "I made him turn the car around, and as soon as we were headed back to Crossroad House, it stopped getting worse. When I stepped inside, the bumps started healing. They're mostly okay now."

But still itchy, because she keeps scratching.

"Stop that." Rose bats her hand away.

Mom grips the back of a chair so hard, her knuckles turn white. "What are you suggesting, Holly? That the *house* wouldn't let you leave the property?"

"*And upon their refusal to converge on home ground as required, a bane of pestilence and plague enjoined their unwilling obedience.*" Ash appears in the doorway, reading off a sheet of notebook paper. He lifts his eyes to us. "That's what I copied from the old journal Flint had in his files."

Mom practically rips the paper out of his hand. She reads the line for herself, then glares at Ash. "*Their* refusal. *Their* obedience. Who are *they*? What's the context for this passage?"

Ash flushes. "There was a transition happening. Some of the family members...uh...refused to come home."

Just like my mother. She keeps glaring, and Ash takes a step backward.

"Mom, it's not his fault." I tug on her sleeve.

She slaps the paper onto the kitchen table and asks me, "Did you leave anything in LJ's room?"

I check that my phone is in my back pocket. "Just the healing bracelets."

"Leave 'em. We have more at home."

That hurts. I've already grown attached to those stones. But Mom whips car keys out of her pocket, turns on her heel, and strides out of the kitchen. I scramble to follow while Holly exclaims to her husband, "Go with her!"

Mom is short, but she can walk really fast when she

wants to. Ash's dad and I hustle to keep up with her as she makes a beeline through the main section of Crossroad House, aiming for the front door. "Mom," I call urgently. "Mom!" I don't like this. She's not listening to what Holly and Ash are saying, or even acknowledging what we're up against.

"I'm going with you, Em," Ash's dad says. "I'm not a Carrefour. It doesn't affect me."

"You'll have to find your way home. I won't be coming back here."

"If you make it to the highway, I'll get out of the car and walk."

Mom glances over her shoulder but doesn't slow down. "That's a long walk."

His expression says he doesn't think he'll have to do it.

He wants to drive, but Mom insists. So he gets into the front passenger seat, and I take the back. Mom fumbles the keys into the ignition and starts the car. I look out the window at the house I so badly wanted to visit, squatting behind us like a poisonous toad. Then my eyes travel up the face of the house to the gabled windows on the third floor, and I remember my uncle's beautiful workshop. *Not poisonous. Poisoned.*

Mom tramps on the gas, and the car lurches over the potholes in the dirt road. Crossroad House disappears behind a parade of trees.

The discomfort hits me before we're five minutes gone, and I know—the way Holly knew—that we need to turn around. "Mom," I say as my stomach starts to rumble. It's not going to be hives for me. *Why is it always stomach stuff?* At least there are no frogs. Just plain old nausea and an urgent need for a bathroom. "Mom! You have to take us back!"

"Hang on, baby. We can make it."

Our poor car bumps over rocks and divots, which doesn't help. My guts feel like they're tying themselves into knots, and I'm so consumed by the misery that it takes me a few seconds to realize the car is slowing. Eventually it stops. Mom throws the driver's door open, leans over, and vomits in the road.

"Emerald," Ash's dad says in the tone of someone trying to reason with an unreasonable person.

She ignores him, breathing heavily. Then she plunges out of the car. I wrap my arms around my middle while she doubles over and pukes some more. But she doesn't give up. Wiping her mouth, she staggers several steps forward.

My mother might be all of five foot nothing, but she's a Carrefour. Defying the family magic, she takes two more steps toward freedom before dropping to her hands and knees in the middle of the road.

Enough is enough. I lower my window and shout, "Mom! Stop it! Get back in the car!" She looks at me, her hair hanging in her pale and sweaty face. "For my sake," I plead, though she's worse off than I am. "Please!" Her shoulders sag in surrender. Stubbornness has gotten her this far, but it won't get us home.

"Em." Ash's dad offers her his hand.

Mom accepts his help. He guides her to the car, tucking her into the passenger's side. She collapses against the door when he takes the driver's seat. As soon as he turns the vehicle around, my symptoms begin to wane—my intestines unknot, my stomach relaxes.

It might be my imagination, but when we reach the driveway, Crossroad House looks triumphant. Almost smug.

By now, the rest of the family knows what's happening. Windy, her mother, Linden, and the teenagers are waiting out front as we drag our curse-ridden bodies out of the car.

River looks at us like we're maggots she discovered in the trash. "But I had plans in town tonight!"

"Not anymore you don't," LJ says, typing on his phone as if canceling his own plans.

The pains in my stomach ease as we make our way to the house, which is wrong, wrong, *wrong*. Yes, I wanted to come here. No, I hadn't wanted to leave.

But every step forward feels like one step closer to a trap.

10

Moonstone

Color: *cloudy white, with shimmering colors*

Magical properties: *aids in divination and meditation*

To recharge: *place under a full moon overnight*

I spend the rest of the day in my uncle's workshop, polishing and sorting stones, and feeling like a fly caught in a web. Mom's there too, trying to read the old journal Ash brought out. By the frowning and muttering and the rubbing of her hand against her forehead, she's not finding what she's looking for.

Uncle Mica taps me on the shoulder and beckons me to his work area, where he's laid out a garnet and an emerald. The emerald is a one-carat stone, emerald cut (which means it's rectangular and leveled like a flat-topped pyramid). The garnet is a cabochon (flat-bottomed with a rounded top), and Uncle Mica has etched a bear's face onto the rounded surface.

I used to hate etched stones until I figured out the etching doesn't hurt them. Uncle Mica's etchings are especially delicate, like fine lace laid over a stone. Garnets boost self-esteem, courage, and hope, and bears are symbols of protection.

The magic Mom and I practice daily calls out the natural inclinations of stones. It takes more effort to create charmed artifacts with specific skills, like amulets, which ward against bad things, and talismans, which attract good things. (Even mundane people without any magic are able to use the charmed items we sell in the shop.)

While I watch, Uncle Mica rolls out a fabric mat with dried flowers embedded in it. On this, he lays the two gems in the center, then chips of mica at the four corners. A small basin of water goes at the top, flanked by white candles, which he lights with a Bic. Plant matter, stones, water, and fire. Earth elements.

He lays his right hand on the mat, his index finger and thumb touching the emerald. Then he gestures for me to copy him. When my fingers mirror his, he nods at me before closing his eyes. He must have his own means of communicating with them, but if he wants me to participate, I'll do it the only way I know. "Lovely emerald," I begin, "so beautiful that an entire cut of gemstone is named after you, protect my mother, another Emerald, against enchantment."

Uncle Mica's eyebrow twitches, and he opens one eye to glance at my mother. Mom doesn't look up from the old journal but mutters, "Told you she was a smooth talker." He smirks briefly before closing his eye again.

The change to the emerald is imperceptible by sight, but I hear the difference in its music, like a single piano note transformed into a rich chord. Under our magical influence, this gem is now charmed as an amulet against enchantment.

Uncle Mica moves his thumb and forefinger to the garnet, and I do the same. "Brave garnet, I hope to be as courageous as you are, to always know when danger is ahead, and to have the luck and wit to avoid it."

The bear-carved garnet roars in response, which is an exceptionally good sign for a talisman meant to bring me courage, luck, and a forewarning of danger. Uncle Mica grins from ear to ear, scooping up both gems and moving them to the station where he will fit them into jewelry settings.

Across the room, Mom closes the worn leather cover with an aggravated sigh.

"So?" I blurt out. "Did you find anything?"

"Just what Ash said. The heir was dying, and some estranged members of the family were summoned home for the transition. They refused the invitation, but were compelled to obedience by *the bane of pestilence and plague*. The phrase isn't explained, and it's never mentioned again. I can't tell if the author was afraid to write too much about it, or if he simply wasn't surprised that it happened."

"Jasper told me the family magic is weakened when members move away and raise their children somewhere else," I say. "Is that why it forced us back?"

"I don't know." Mom purses her lips. "But I called your school and told them you'd be on an extended absence due to a family emergency."

I've had a couple of texts from friends asking where I am. I told them there'd been a death in the family. I didn't mention we were hoping for another one. I don't want to answer their follow-up questions. Most of my friends believe in magic at least a little—enough to wear a talisman or hang a crystal—but Crossroad House and our reasons for being here feel like private things.

Uncle Mica returns holding a silver chain necklace, displaying the attached garnet pendant against the palm of his other hand.

"It's beautiful! Thank you!"

His response is to drape it around my neck and fasten the clasp. When the stone settles against me, it roars a soft hello.

Then, with a flourish, Mica produces the second necklace. He has set the emerald in filigree surrounded by chips of hematite, obsidian, and tiger's-eye—all protective stones. Mom takes the amulet into her hands to examine, but gives him a look. "You didn't have to make this. Garnet's the one in danger, not me."

Her brother raises a doubtful eyebrow. He points at Mom, then brushes his hands together, driving his right hand away from himself in a *getting-out-of-here* gesture. I don't know what he means, but he and Mom had years to get the hang of nonverbal communication, and she apparently hasn't lost her touch in the time they've been apart. "You think I'm a target because I left?" He looks pointedly at the old journal, then back at her. She exhales to acknowledge his point. "In that case, you'd better make one for Rose, too."

Uncle Mica shoots me a conspiratorial wink, as if to say, *Who does she think she's dealing with?* Out of a pocket, he produces a polished rose quartz which will no doubt soon become an amulet for our cousin. Uncle Mica is one step ahead of us.

Mom gives in and clasps the necklace around her neck. "You didn't have to use such a valuable emerald, you know." Uncle Mica rolls his eyes expressively, indicating that she ought to know there is no emerald more valuable than his sister, Emerald.

I smile. Communicating with my uncle is easier than I thought.

That evening, after supper, I wrap my hand around my garnet bear talisman for comfort when Mom leads me to the sunroom. The black sky outside has turned the three walls of windows into mirrors.

Windy is already there, lighting white and black candles on the side tables and window ledges. Each wick sparks a twin in the reflective glass until the room is aglow with candlelight, real and replicated.

Mom squeezes my hand. "Are you sure you're okay with this?"

It's important for me to know what kind of danger I'm in. I mean, if someone had told Sleeping Beauty to stay away from spinning wheels, she probably wouldn't have gotten her finger pricked. But I'm nervous. I don't want to say that, so I just nod.

"There's nothing to be afraid of," Windy assures us, gesturing for me to sit across from her at a round glass table where a silver basin of water awaits. "I'll do all the work."

She lays objects around the basin: milky moonstones, jagged slivers of flint, and tiny cloth bags tied with string. "Tea leaves," she says when she notices me eyeing them. "Traditional in fortune-casting."

Water, fire, plants, and stone. Mom adds air—which complements water—by cranking open one of the windows. A cold breeze rushes in, threatening the candles, but Windy waggles her fingers and whispers, "Away!" The current of air, diverted by her command, shifts away from the perimeter of tiny flames.

"Garnet," Windy says next, "we'll need a small piece of you to complete the spell." My eyes jump to her in alarm, and she laughs. "Some hair or fingernail clippings."

I turn in my seat to stare at Mom. "How did you get that before I was born?"

Windy answers for her. "We used your mother's hair. It was *her* augury we cast. But it was *about* you."

Mom comes over, scissors in hand, waiting for me to give up part of myself. Fingernail clippings? Eww. I hold up a lock of my hair instead and Mom clips it.

A shiver runs down my back. I remind myself that what we're doing is no different from what Uncle Mica and I did this afternoon. No different from Windy directing the current of air moments ago. Even though it *feels* different.

Windy's gift for divination is rare and special and, to me, mysterious. Not every Carrefour gets an extra gift unrelated to their talent with earth elements. In fact, it makes Windy an excellent candidate for the family heir, so I'm not sure why everyone assumes the title will go to Linden— unless they don't believe Jasper will choose a woman. I don't know if there's ever been a female Carrefour heir, but I'm betting not. People who make their kids live in the attic don't sound like they'd be into gender equality.

Mom places my snipped-off ends in Windy's hands, who casts them over the basin of water. Then she eases back in her chair, relaxes her shoulders, and places her hands on either side of the basin. Closing her eyes, she whispers, "Wind and water, fire and stone, green vegetation that gives us life. I beseech you. Guide me and show me what this child, Garnet, needs to know." Her eyes open, and she gazes into the water.

I look too, and see...Water. With bits of my hair floating on top.

Mom paces off to the side, chewing her nails.

Meanwhile, Windy stares at the surface of the water, its reflection enhancing the golden hue of her skin. Her irises dart back and forth. Her pupils expand, like she's watching a show on a TV screen. I'm aware of my heart rate jumping, my breath becoming ragged...

A minute passes, maybe more. Finally, Windy jerks upright and splashes her fingers across the water like she's dismissing an app on her phone.

Mom rushes forward and grips the back of my chair. "Well?"

Windy raises her eyes. Her pupils are still dilated. "It's the same, Em. Exactly as before. I see her walking through the gateposts of Old House—and she disappears."

Mom sags. "The same?"

"Yes. But, Em." Unexpectedly, Windy grabs my hands. "Last time, I saw a girl, and we assumed it was your child.

This time, it's definitely Garnet. At *this* age. I am seeing something that happens *this* fall, to *this* child."

My instinct is to yank my hands away. But they're numb.

I can't see Mom's expression. She's behind me while Windy speaks, sounding urgent. "Don't panic. Those ruins might be a vortex for life energy, but you'll have every single Carrefour working to help you protect her."

This is why Mom left Crossroad House. I mean, I knew all along that the augury was the reason, but now I *feel* it. She didn't leave home after the fire, after her mother's death. But when Windy predicted this fate for *me*, she fled and didn't return until forced to.

I lick my dry lips. "Windy." My voice comes out as a croak, and Windy turns her green gaze back to me. "How many times has a person avoided an augury you cast for them?"

She tries to form an answer that will reassure me. I see her sorting through possible responses. But her hesitation tells me everything.

You know about the spinning wheel, Sleeping Beauty. But can you avoid getting pricked?

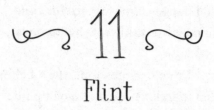

Flint

Color: *black, brown, or gray*

Magical properties: *helps one's spiritual energy face the past*

To recharge: *polish to a high gloss*

In the morning, Mom and I get ready for Uncle Flint's funeral. We don't talk about the augury. What is there to say? Plus, words have power.

That doesn't stop River from putting my fate into words when she drops off funeral-appropriate clothes. "My mother told me about the augury," she says, passing a pile of dark-colored fabric and shoes into my arms. "Be careful." I'm a little touched by her concern until she adds, "If Old House gobbles up your life energy and gives it to Jasper, we'll never be rid of him."

That is...not helpful. She vanishes before I can come up with a good retort.

I put on the clothes she loaned me, and Mom wears what Windy sent for her. When we leave our borrowed room, Mom grabs my hand and won't let go.

On our way downstairs to get breakfast, we hear hammering from inside the library. We peer through the doorway and see Ash's dad hammering plywood boards across one of the windows.

"What happened?" Mom asks.

"A branch busted through the glass last night. From that maple tree out front."

Mom frowns. "I didn't hear a storm."

He shrugs. "Must've been a stray gust of wind. Weirder things have happened here."

"This house is a disaster," Mom mutters, tugging on my hand.

An hour later, the family gathers in the front parlor. I was worried about seeing my first dead body, but the casket is closed.

The men from the funeral home are the only non-Carrefours present. No neighbors. No friends. Linden's "ex"-wife, Victoria, comes, but she stands on the opposite side of the room from him, like they're trying to fool the house.

Linden raises an eyebrow at Mom. "Is Mica coming?" Mom shakes her head, and Linden gives a tiny grunt, like he didn't expect anything different but had to ask. "Then let's begin."

Jasper rises from a chair—slowly and with a lot of help from his cane. LJ offers an arm, but Jasper shakes his head. He shuffles to the coffin, which is set on a stand in the middle of the room, and places a hand on top of it. Then, to my surprise, Jasper looks at me and glances pointedly at his own hand, before turning to everyone else.

The Carrefour Diamond shines in a clean setting, the carved enamel band free of dirt.

Ha! I shamed him into cleaning the ring! Mom scowls at him for paying me special attention.

Jasper begins the service by reciting the basics of his son's life. He shares a few stories about Flint as a boy. Some of them might've been funny if everybody in the room wasn't wishing we were attending *Jasper's* funeral. Only Linden laughs at the right places. Only Tempest, the last of Flint's generation, cries. Jasper tires quickly. When returning to his seat, he accepts LJ's help.

Next, every member of the family except me shares a memory of Flint. Mom talks about learning the subtleties of stone magic from her uncle when she was a child. Holly mentions his dry sense of humor. "It was hard to tell if he was joking or not...until he gave you that wink." Family members smile and nod in agreement.

"He had style for an old guy," River says. "Those matching pocket squares and socks killed me."

Even Oak speaks up. "He said I was a little dickens. Then he gave me a toffee!"

Several people mention Flint's passion for keeping records of the family history. No one brings up the fire.

Linden reads from an old Bible. Holly—now blemish-free—opens the Family Book and enters Flint's death date. Laying the pen aside, she hesitates, leans closer to the giant tome, and rubs her finger against the page. She gazes around the room, looking puzzled, before closing the Book.

The funeral home men carry the casket out of the parlor, through the front door, and down the concrete steps.

Everyone but Jasper lines up behind them and walks across the brown, unkempt grass to the family cemetery.

It seems creepy to bury family on the property, where you can see the gravestones out your bedroom window. I suppose people whose gifts come from the earth might want to be put to rest in that same earth, but I keep remembering what Jasper said about building over the crossroad, raising children in that structure, and keeping family close to fuel the power. It feels like we're recycling Uncle Flint.

The procession enters the cemetery through a crumbling gate. I glance toward the woods that lie between us and the stone pillars marking the path to the ruins of Old House. Mom's grip on my hand tightens so that my fingertips turn white. Does she think I'm going to make a dash for the woods if she lets go? It's not like this is a movie where the main character sneaks off to explore the forbidden ruins as soon as possible. I am *never* going there.

Then I think about the frogs.

Holly's hives.

The force that compelled my mother back to the house yesterday.

The fact that the family magic may have dragged me here on purpose to give my life energy to the dying heir.

Crossroad House has ways of making you do things you don't want to do. A chill runs down my spine, and I don't complain about my mother cutting off the circulation to my fingers.

Uncle Flint's grave lies next to his sister's. Her gravestone reads OPAL CARREFOUR ~ DAUGHTER, SISTER, WIFE,

MOTHER. Grandmother, too, only she didn't live to see that. On the other side of her grave is the grave of my grandfather, deceased five years before his wife. His stone says JOHN BLAKE. It seems that none of the Carrefour women take their husbands' names.

Linden makes a few remarks at the graveside, and the funeral home men hand everyone a cut flower to place on the casket. Afterward, we leave the professionals to finish their job and trek back to the house for the funeral dinner. LJ's mother breaks from the group at the front steps, giving her son a quick hug before walking to her car.

The table in the dining room has been set for thirteen people—the twelve of us who attended the funeral and one more for Uncle Mica, even though no one expects him to come down from the attic.

While Holly escorts Jasper to his place and the adults (plus the ever-helpful LJ) carry platters from the kitchen, I slip away to the downstairs powder room to wash my hands. As I exit the room, a breeze of fresh air catches my attention.

The sliding glass door that leads to the falling-down porch is open several inches. I've never seen it open before. Someone must have cracked the door for air while the cooking was happening in the kitchen. Grasping the handle with both hands to close it, I stop when I see what's on the other side of the glass.

The lumbering gray clouds that presided over Uncle Flint's burial have given way to a gorgeous blue sky. Sunlight splashes the porch, illuminating chairs and a glider that must've been dragged out of storage. Unease prickles my skin. Why put furniture on a porch that's falling apart—at a time of year when no one wants to sit outside?

Slipping through the crack, I step gingerly onto the porch floorboards. Ash said it was dangerous, but if I'm destined to disappear between the gates of Old House, the porch roof isn't going to fall on my head. The boards feel solid beneath my feet, and when I look up, the roof is intact. When did it get fixed?

Something is off. I need to tell someone—Mom, Windy, Linden—that bad magic is happening out here. But when I make up my mind to turn around, my body walks forward instead. Right, left, right, left. My legs take steps without my permission, propelling me across the porch, down a couple of steps, and onto the lawn.

The sound of splashing water greets me as I approach the abandoned goldfish pond. Except, it's not abandoned. A vigorous stream of water tumbles down an artificial waterfall into a stone-lined pond where a couple of dozen fish in hues of gold, red, and mottled blue dance in the frothy water.

Am I dreaming? Did I fall asleep during Uncle Flint's funeral? Or has the family magic decided today is the day I walk through the gates of Old House? Windy might have mentioned I was wearing her daughter's clothes in her vision!

Then I notice I'm not wearing the shoes and skirt River gave me. As I fight for control of my feet, I see they are inserted into jelly flip-flops, my bare legs exposed to the mid-thigh by cutoff jeans shorts.

These are not my clothes. Those are not my legs and feet!

Someone shrieks.

I try to turn around and get back to the house, but the stupid feet attached to these stupid legs keep walking toward the sound of the scream. Not toward Old House, thankfully, but across a conspicuously neat green lawn to the spot where the yard drops off. Here my body stops and looks down the hill.

The rectangular cement pool is a blue gem in the sunlight, like the diamond on Jasper's ring. Around its perimeter, three teenage girls lie, sunning themselves.

Two boys wrestle on the diving board, one light-skinned, one dark olive, each of them shouting and laughing.

While I watch, the light-skinned boy pushes the other one into the water, then runs up and down the diving board, pumping his arms in victory. The second boy pops up seconds later, grabbing the diving board with one hand and trying to reach the ankles of his opponent with the other.

One of the girls beside the pool sits up on her lounge chair, her hand holding a wide-brimmed sun hat on her blond head. "Hey there!" she calls to me.

If I was in control of my knees, they would've collapsed. The girl's face is stunningly familiar, and her ashen hair is cut in the style that got famous on the TV show *Friends*.

"Come on down!" the girl shouts in Mom's voice. "The water's fine!"

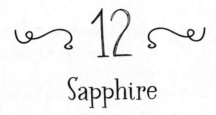

Sapphire

Color: *pale to midnight blue*

Magical properties: *amplifies psychic powers,*
facilitates astral projection

To recharge: *cover in sea salt*

The legs attached to my body accept the invitation, propelling me down a set of stone steps to the lower yard. This must be a dream. But I feel the sunlight on my skin and the sticky humidity of a summer day.

Down by the pool, my mother—the teenage Emerald—watches me descend the hill. *Does she know who I am?* I don't know how everything works at Crossroad House. Maybe residents welcome visitors from the future on a regular basis.

On the chair next to Mom, stretched out in the sun, lies a girl with a golden tan and a flipped-up bob of black hair. Windy. Teenage Holly lounges nearby, strawberry-blond curls restrained on the top of her head with a plastic clip. Their swimsuits and hairstyles match the only photo Mom kept from Crossroad House. "Do you have a suit, Tana?" Emerald asks.

"No." The person who answers is me. Well, not me. The voice is too high and breathy. But it's coming from the body I'm looking out of.

"Brand," says Emerald, addressing the boy bobbing in the pool. "Why didn't you tell your sister to bring a bathing suit?"

"I thought she was going to stay with Rose."

My head turns to stare at him. Who is he?

Whoever Brand is, he doesn't like my expression. "Don't look at me like that. If you wanted to swim, you should have said so."

The girl steps my body closer to the pool and replies, rather petulantly, "You didn't give me the choice." Her reflection appears in the water: silky dark hair and a Mediterranean complexion, much like her brother. She's thinner and more delicate than I am, dressed in frayed jeans shorts and a tank top, but the girl possessing me is about my age. Or am I possessing her?

"Where *is* Rose?" Holly asks.

"Reading a book and ignoring me," Tana answers.

"The least she could do is loan you a suit." The boy who'd been wrestling Brand is now straddling the diving board. "Do you want me to ask her to find one for you?"

Tana looks him directly in the face for the first time. It's Uncle Mica! Long hair hangs almost to his shoulders in wet strands. His face is unscarred. If this is the summer of 1998—and it must be, by the haircuts on my mom and her cousins—it's only a few weeks before the fire that will cost three lives and permanently injure two others.

"Earth to Tana!" Mica says, laughing. "D'ya want Rose to loan you a bathing suit?"

Can I warn them? Is that why the house magic brought me here?

As hard as I can, I try to make this girl speak. *Hello. I'm not Tana. I'm Emerald's daughter come from the future to warn you about a terrible tragedy....*

Tana answers, "No. It looks like rain." She lifts her gaze to clouds hovering over the distant woods. Then she pouts at her brother. "You should have asked me earlier."

A jolt hits me. My father must have been olive-skinned with dark hair for me to turn out with my coloring. Could this boy be...

"It's not going to rain on us." Windy holds up a bottle of tanning oil. "Brand, would you rub this on my back?"

"Sure thing!" Brand practically throws himself out of the pool to run over and sit on the lounge chair beside Windy.

Ohhh...he's Windy's boyfriend. Besides, Mom was in her twenties when she met the archaeology student who became my father. In 1998, she was only sixteen.

"Don't bother," Mica says. "Rain *is* coming, Win."

Sun still shines on the pool, but over the woods, the sky has darkened to purple.

Windy rises from her lounge chair. "Wanna bet?"

A garden hose hangs over the side of the pool, like it'd been used to top off the water. Windy scoops it up and turns it on. Walking around the pool, she waves the head of the hose like a conductor with a baton, casting out streaming arcs of water in curves and loops. Her lips move, although I can't hear what she's saying. Rainbow prisms appear in the spray as if she's constructing a dome of stained glass. She finishes her circuit just as the sky darkens and a wall of rain heads toward us. Windy turns off the hose and faces the deluge defiantly.

The rain diverts around both sides of the pool and reunites on the far end. All around us, fat drops flatten the grass, but our area remains dry.

"Whoooa," Brand says in a low voice.

"Show-off," Mica grumbles good-naturedly, still perched on the diving board.

"Garnet!"

I startle to hear my name and whirl around, seeking the source.

River stands at the top of the hill. And she's not standing in the rain.

The grass between us is ragged and brown. The stone steps leading up the hill are broken, and I am wearing black flats and a black skirt. When I look behind me, the pool is nothing but a cement pit in the ground.

The teens are gone, and so is any chance to warn them.

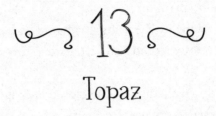

Topaz

Color: *golden yellow to orange-yellow*

Magical properties: *protects against untimely death and negative magic*

To recharge: *hold under running water*

"What were you doing down there?" River demands, hands on her hips.

I have no answer. There *is* no answer that makes sense.

It was like a waking dream. My body really did walk down to the pool, even though it didn't seem to be my body at the time. As I follow River back into the house—which we enter by way of the sunroom because *of course* the porch is still falling down and the sliding glass door is closed—I wonder how to explain what happened.

Inside, River almost collides with Mom, who's barreling down the main hallway from the direction of the staircase, looking wild-eyed. "She's not upstairs!"

"I'm here, Mom." I step out from behind my cousin.

"She was outside," River says with a shrug that suggests she can't explain me.

Mom grabs me by the arms, the panic on her face turning to anger. "Why would you be outside? Where were you going?"

I glance down the hall at the closed sliding glass door. "I just...you see, there was fresh air..."

Immediately, her expression changes. "Oh, baby. Your first funeral." She pulls me into a hug. "Of course you needed fresh air. I should have realized."

Overcome with emotion, and a side of hallucination, after attending my first funeral? I don't think so. "Mom," I begin, pulling away from her hug, "that picture we have on the wall back home, of you and Holly and Windy by the pool...What do you remember about that day?"

"What?" Mom says, looking deeply puzzled by the question.

Before I can explain—*How? Where do I start?*—Holly sticks her head out of the dining room. "Are you two ready? Jasper's getting cranky."

Mom rolls her eyes and steers me through the doorway. "Heaven forbid we keep His Highness waiting."

Inside, the entire Carrefour clan, minus Uncle Mica, is staring at me, some of them impatiently because I held up their dinner. I can't ask about time travel right now. It's too insane.

Instead, I slide into an empty chair and drop my napkin in my lap like a well-mannered Carrefour who doesn't randomly travel to the past for no reason at all.

❧

Halfway through dinner, Jasper falls asleep in his chair. Conversation around the dining table fumbles to a halt.

"Somebody get a mirror and check for breathing," Rose mutters.

Holly walks to the head of the table. "Uncle Jasper." She pats his shoulder. He startles awake and looks around, confused. His shaggy eyebrows rumple in suspicion, like he doesn't trust what we were up to while his guard was down. "Let me take you to your room."

Jasper rises stiffly. His knuckles tighten around his cane, and he grumbles under his breath. "The chicken was dry, and the potatoes were lumpy."

"Well, that's a shame. I'll brew that bergamot-ginger tea you like and bring it up to you."

No one speaks while Holly escorts Jasper from the room. We fix our attention on our food as if it might disappear if we don't keep our forks moving, but as soon as he's out of earshot, River exclaims, "How long are we stuck here? I have a life!"

"You mean, you *had* a life," Rose counters, fingering a rose quartz pendant carved in the shape of a rose—the amulet Uncle Mica made for her.

"No, seriously," River insists, turning to her mother. "My friends are going to know something's wrong if I never leave the house."

"Why don't you invite them here?" I suggest. "Since you can't...go...there." My voice trails off when everyone stares at me like I've sprouted two heads.

Rose answers sharply. "We don't bring people we care about to this place! Not during a transition." She flashes me her engagement ring so I'll know exactly who she's talking about. Beside her, LJ drops his head and stares at his plate. I remember that his mother didn't even stay for dinner.

"To answer your question, River…" Linden wipes his mouth fussily with his napkin and carefully folds it before continuing. "We don't know how long this will last. No one was trapped on the property the last time Jasper was sick."

"It didn't happen during the transition from Old Linden to Jasper, either," Windy's mother declares. "Of course, the entire family lived on the premises back then. No one had to be coerced into coming and forced to stay."

Mom scowls. "Are you blaming *me* for our predicament?"

"Maybe we should all calm down," Ash's dad quietly suggests.

"Says the one person who can get in the car and drive away," Windy mutters, flinging her napkin to the table, where it lands beside Linden's perfectly folded one.

I don't like that the adults don't know what's going on. It doesn't give me much confidence in their ability to protect me from the fate in the augury. They don't even know where I was half an hour ago. What a change from those laughing, carefree teens to this group of frightened, trapped people!

Tossing her bright burgundy hair over her shoulder, Rose addresses the group. "So are we going to sit here and wait for him to die?"

"Are you suggesting there's something else we can do?" Linden asks.

Rose lifts her chin. "Maybe."

Everyone glances uneasily at everyone else. Is she hinting at what I think she is?

"Dark deeds have dark consequences," Windy's mother intones ominously. "And earth magic has a long memory."

"I was only joking, Tempest," Rose snaps at the older woman, sounding as far from joking as one can possibly get.

❧

After dinner, the adults clean up. LJ volunteers to help, but Windy says, "You kids go outside. It's going to rain for the next three days, and you'll be cooped up in the house."

If anyone else said that, I'd assume they'd checked Weather.com. But after what I saw—dreamed? hallucinated?—I'm pretty sure Windy doesn't need the help of a weatherman.

"Garnet, wanna see me fly my copter?" Oak bounces up and down.

"Okay."

Ash and I end up sitting on the sunroom stoop while Oak flies his remote-control helicopter. River stands apart from us, sending texts on her phone and cursing when they don't go through. LJ enthusiastically cheers on Oak's flying skills.

I consider telling my cousins what happened to me before the funeral dinner. Maybe they'll say, *Oh, we visit our teenage parents all the time.* Maybe it's not a big deal, although you'd think someone would have mentioned it by now. Plus, I didn't visit the past as myself. I saw it through the eyes of some girl named Tana.

A girl who was visiting Crossroad House in the summer of 1998...

LJ kicks one of the rocks on the lip of the abandoned goldfish pond. "When my dad's in charge, he's going to bulldoze this. Fill in that old swimming pool and pull down the porch. He wants to rebuild the wing that burned. We could use the extra bedrooms, and a billiard room down-stairs would be cool."

Beside me, Ash shudders. I already know what he thinks about the burned wing. What about Mom and Uncle Mica? Has Linden considered how they feel about re-creating the place where their mother died?

River looks up from her phone. "What makes you so sure your dad will be the next heir?"

"Who else? You don't really think your mom stands a chance, do you?"

"I think she's a better choice than your father."

"River!" Oak crashes into her. "Help me! It's stuck!"

We look up. Oak landed his helicopter on the half-collapsed porch roof and is now frantically jiggling the switch on his remote, trying to make it lift off. I'm surprised he asked River for help instead of his brother...until she takes the device and works the toggle, moving her lips the way Windy did when sheltering the swimming pool from the rain.

"My father is a businessman," LJ says, frowning. "He has degrees in accounting and finance. No offense, River, but your mom's basically a fortune-teller."

Clearly, the tension from the funeral dinner has fol-lowed us outside.

"I don't take offense over my mother's *gift*." River hands the remote back to Oak. "Sorry. It's caught on some-thing. I don't want to force it. I might break it."

Oak wails. "But I want my copter!"

Ash jumps up. "I'll get Dad to bring the ladder." He jogs across the yard, like he's eager to escape the conversation. Part of me wants to go with him, but the other part is hungry for the family gossip I've been missing my whole life, so I stay put.

River faces off against her cousin. "Fact is, we could use a woman heir for a change. One who leads us forward instead of backward. Your father licks Jasper's boots so much, we might as well call him New Jasper."

"I resent that," LJ says, his face flushing. "Besides, Jasper has been a good leader to this family. We've done well under his guidance...until he got sick."

"Tell that to the people who died in 1998 so he could live," River retorts. "Tell it to—" Her gaze glides toward me, and I expect her to say: *Tell it to Garnet, who's going to get* eaten *by Old House.* But her eyes pass me and sweep the area. "Where's Oak?"

The remote control for the helicopter is lying on the ground, but Ash's rambunctious little brother is nowhere to be seen.

"Oak!" LJ raises his voice. "Where are you?"

"Getting my copter!"

We look up at the house. A second-floor window opens, and Oak climbs out onto the dilapidated porch roof.

14

Hematite

Color: *brown, reddish brown, black, or steel gray*

Magical properties: *reduces excessive bleeding, assists in clotting*

To recharge: *tumble amid clear quartz crystals*

"Oak!" River yells. "Get down from there!"

LJ is more precise. "Go back through the window!"

"Soon as I get my copter." Oak edges sideways down the roof, his eyes fixed on the toy.

"No, Oak! Go inside!" I shout, backing several steps away from the house to get a better view. Then I notice something.

To reach the porch roof, Oak has climbed out a window in the second-floor hallway. Jasper's bedroom juts out from that hallway, and Jasper himself stands in the window with the best view of Oak's predicament. There's no way he missed Oak opening the hall window and climbing out. Even if he's too frail to stop the boy, he could've raised an alarm. Instead, he chose to *watch*. My hands clench.

"Easy does it." LJ pats the air with both hands. "If you can't reach it—"

"Got it!" Oak's hand closes on one of the rotor blades, and then his legs break through the roof. He screams.

The roof collapses in slow motion. The structure leans inward, where the helicopter was caught and where Oak fell through. Shingles break away, wood splinters, and it looks like Oak's small body is going to disappear amid the destruction.

River gestures with her hands and yells, "To me!"

Instead of falling straight down with the rest of the roof, Oak shoots forward, propelled by a concentrated gust of wind. LJ takes two steps backward, one to the left, and catches the child like he's an oversized football. I want to cheer and clap my hands, but I don't. There's too much blood.

LJ lays Oak on the ground and clamps his hands around the boy's leg. He looks at River, who's running toward the house screaming for help. Then his eyes land on me. "Take off my belt," he orders.

I wrap my arms around his waist to undo his buckle and pull the belt free. "Tie it around his thigh," he directs me. "No, higher. There. Now tighten it."

My hands shake, costing me precious seconds as I slip the end of the belt through the buckle and pull on it while Oak sobs hysterically.

"Tighter," LJ orders.

My stomach flip-flops, but I pull the belt with all my strength.

"That's it. Good job, Garnet. Good job."

The adults appear, drawn by River's screams. Two of them scoop Oak off the ground. Mom's hands replace LJ's, putting pressure on the wound. Holly runs alongside her injured son, chanting, "Mommy's here, Mommy's here!"

Ash and his father arrive just in time to see them all disappear into the house. Ash's dad drops his end of the ladder and runs after the others, hollering at Ash to *"Stay here!"* Poor Ash gapes after his brother.

I look up at the second floor. Jasper is gone. Is he rushing downstairs to make sure his great-grandnephew is okay? I doubt it. Furiously, I open my mouth to denounce the soul-sucking old vampire. Before I can, River collapses onto the brown grass and covers her face, shoulders shaking.

LJ holds his bloody hands out and looks around, as if searching for a towel. With none to be found, he wipes them on the grass. Then he shuffles over to River and sinks down. He sits close enough to provide solidarity, never mind that they'd been arguing minutes earlier. To my surprise, I find myself drawn to sit on River's other side. Ash abandons the ladder and joins us.

Eventually River wipes her eyes and opens her arms to Ash, offering a hug. He takes it, hiding his face from everyone. "If you tell anybody I cried, I'll kill you all," she says.

"Don't worry." LJ loud-whispers at me, "I know at least six things about River worth killing me for, or so she says, but I'm seventy-five-percent sure she won't do it." He smiles. "You did a good job, Garnet. You're a Carrefour, through and through."

I'm embarrassed by the rush of pride I feel at his words. "I felt sick. Like I might throw up or pass out."

"So did I," he admits.

Any other family would call 911. But Oak can't be taken to the hospital. Luckily, Holly is a trained nurse, and Carrefour magic is more than capable of handling an injury like this one.

When I peek at Oak later, his leg has been stitched and bandaged with a poultice by Holly. Over the bandage, Mom has laid a fine silver mesh dotted with hematite for clotting. She must have gotten it from Uncle Mica. Meanwhile, Oak is grumbling that he doesn't want the tea Rose is trying to give him.

"Drink it," Rose says, "or I'll get a funnel and pour it in."

Oak looks to his mother for rescue, but Holly says, "She'll do it."

Oak drinks the tea.

I back out of the room and bump into Ash peeking in. "How is he?" he asks.

I'm surprised he doesn't check for himself. Then I remember how he reacted to the blood. "He'll be okay. The hardest part will be keeping him still while he heals."

Ash visibly relaxes. "That's what Aunt Rose's tea is for, to knock him out."

Mom exits Oak's room, closing the door behind her. "We should get out of their way. There's nothing more our stone magic can do."

Ash looks forlorn, probably thinking there's nothing his flower magic can do, either. "Okay if I come with you?" he asks. "We could see if Netflix is working."

"Good idea," Mom says, steering both of us. She's

probably thinking what a relief it'll be to park me in front of a TV instead of wondering if I've wandered outside for "fresh air" again.

So I wait until she's left us in the TV room before I say to Ash, "Actually, I was wondering if I could look at the Family Book. Is that allowed?"

"Sure." He perks up, as if the Family Book is more interesting than the newest show on Netflix.

When it's not being used at funerals or to register new members of the family, the Book rests on its pedestal in the library. It's so old, I handle each page like it might disintegrate in my hands—although I bet someone has put preservation spells on them.

The Book begins with Diamon Carrefour, the ancestor who came from Europe and built Old House on an intersection of ley lines in the 1700s. One of the first things I notice is that spouses aren't listed in the Book. Non-Carrefours simply don't matter to this record, descendants springing from a single parent like Athena out of Zeus's head.

Even without spouses, the family tree gets complicated. Tracking one generation to the next becomes difficult as I turn the pages. But then, as Jasper mentioned, the family grows thin. Branches die off or move away, until the family is reduced to the 1874 Linden. Old Linden. From this one man, it branches out again.

My eyes drift from the Family Book to the painting of Old Linden and his family. For the first time, I pay attention to the children standing off to the side and connect them with the names and dates in the book. "Those two died young." At the ages of five and four, to be precise.

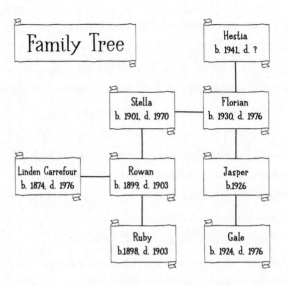

Family Tree

			Hestia b. 1941, d. ?
	Stella b. 1901, d. 1970	Florian b. 1930, d. 1976	
Linden Carrefour b. 1874, d. 1976	Rowan b. 1899, d. 1903	Jasper b.1926	
	Ruby b.1898, d. 1903	Gale b. 1924, d. 1976	

They appear slightly younger than that in the painting: a solemn-eyed little girl holding the hand of her toddler brother.

"Ruby and Rowan? Yeah, they did. Only Stella lived to grow up. She was pretty fascinating."

"The baby?" She's barely a smudge of peach brushstrokes buried in ivory cloth.

"She's in this painting, too." Ash points to the one on the other side of the fireplace, the woman with four children. "That's her. Jasper's mother. He's the boy—"

"—with the hairy eyebrows." Even in the painting, he glares down at us. "What's so fascinating about Stella?"

"She was exceptionally gifted and mastered all the earth elements. She dreamed she'd have four children who would establish four family lines dedicated to specific talents. Carrefour legend says that when Stella held each of her children in her arms, she knew what their gift would be and named them accordingly. Before that, it was pretty random which elements a Carrefour might favor, and people's names didn't line up with their talents. But the descendants of Stella's children have bred true."

I glance back at the Family Book to reference Stella's children. The oldest, Gale, would have been master of air and water. Jasper, of course, works with stones. Florian would have summoned magic out of plants, and their sister Hestia would have...what?

"What's the fire talent like?" I ask.

"Manipulation of flame, I guess. Flint mentioned something about visions, but no one has seen that talent in action since Hestia ran away in 1976. Jasper would know."

I lean over the Book again, scanning the dates beneath people's names. "The last transition occurred in 1976, right? Old Linden died—whoa, he was a hundred and two years old—and Jasper became the heir. Jasper's brothers died earlier that year and now you're saying Hestia left too?"

"It wasn't just his brothers. In the spring of 1976, the wives of Gale, Jasper, and Florian died from botulism after eating home-canned fruit."

"Spouses first." I shiver. "Then the family members?"

Ash nods. "Gale and Jasper were repairing the roof when Gale fell off a ladder and broke his neck. Then Florian died in a boating accident. Jasper was the only witness."

"And Hestia..." The chill increases, running up my arms.

"Figured out she was next and ran off, if she was smart.

Hey, what's this?" Ash exclaims suddenly, rubbing his finger on the page. "Does this look like a bloodstain to you?"

"There are bloodstains *all over* this book." Every name is handwritten in the shaky script of a child guided by an adult, with a smudge of blood beside it. But Ash is referring to a smear an inch below Hestia's signature. "Maybe somebody dripped where they weren't supposed to."

"No. This mark wasn't here when you signed. I'm sure of it."

"Then it happened today."

"You mean someone got a paper cut during the funeral?"

I recall Holly looking puzzled at this same page during the service, and my eyes drift toward the window broken in the night by a flying tree branch. A thought occurs to me—but someone breaking into the house to bleed on the Family Book is even wilder than my trip to 1998. "Maybe it's a coincidence. Most of the things in this house are stained."

He sighs. "True."

Mysterious stains aside, this section of the family tree gives me the creeps. I look at Stella's children in the painting and blurt out what I'm thinking. "Did the *house* bump off Gale and Florian to preserve the life of the *old* heir? Or did *Jasper* get rid of his competition to be the *new* heir?"

Ash lifts both hands, palms up, as if weighing two things that are about the same. "Flint thought it was the first one, but he was Jasper's son and inclined to defend him. Personally? I think Jasper killed both his brothers to become the Carrefour heir. And I don't believe Hestia escaped either."

15

Amethyst

Color: *lilac and lavender to deep purple*

Magical properties: *wards against danger, both physical and psychic*

To recharge: *bathe in warm water, then place among hematite*

The next morning, I wake with a burning desire to visit the family cemetery.

Usually I wake up thinking about my options for breakfast. Gravestones seem like a strange alternative, but I've been dreaming about them all night.

Yesterday evening, I went through the Family Book again on my own. Ash said that every time the family heir weakens, other people die, but, looking through the book, I couldn't find much evidence of that.

First of all, the book didn't identify the people designated as heirs, so I had to look for years with multiple deaths. I found several years when more than one Carrefour died, but it was usually two or three old people, not five or six relatively young ones. Not until 1976 and 1998.

I started wondering if Ash had it wrong—or if this phenomenon was a fairly recent development, something that began in the twentieth century. Then I remembered that spouses are often included in the casualties, and spouses aren't listed in the Book. But they *are* buried in the cemetery. I noticed that at Flint's service. If I go looking, will I find other victims of Carrefour magic?

I'm not sure why it matters to me. I guess I feel that the better I understand what happens during a transition of power, the better I can try to avoid the fate in Windy's augury.

I stop in the kitchen for a bowl of cereal first because *priorities*! Mom's already there with a mug of coffee, and Windy appears a few minutes later, coming from the door that leads to Ash's family's wing. "How's Oak?" Mom asks.

"Doing well. Holly bribed him with three new video games to stay in bed. Thank the earth magic for same-day delivery!"

"Has anyone checked on Jasper this morning?"

"I did." Windy pours herself a cup of coffee. "He's SND. Still Not Dead."

"Windy!" Mom cuts her eyes toward me.

"What? Oak could've died yesterday. Then we would've seen Jasper strutting around, looking stronger for a few days. Garnet knows what's going on now, Em."

Mom's face flushes when she looks at me. "It wasn't always like this. When Jasper was healthy, the house was a healthy place to be. Growing up here was like living in a magical paradise. I didn't want to tell you what it's become. I didn't want to face it myself." Mom puts her hands over her face. "I'm sorry."

"It's okay, Mom. I get it." I get it more than she knows, thanks to my vision by the pool. Maybe that's why the house showed it to me. So I could understand my mom and forgive her for keeping secrets.

"Stay on guard," Windy says. "We're not out of this until Jasper passes on the ring."

"Is that all he has to do? Give away the ring?" I ask.

"He has to formally name a successor," Mom says, lowering her hands. "Giving away the ring is part of the ceremony. Control of the family magic passes to the designated heir, and Jasper will pass on after that."

"I don't suppose we can *take* the ring from him?" Is that what Rose meant at dinner yesterday—or was she suggesting worse?

Windy huffs. "If it was that easy, I would've wrestled the ring off him myself."

I have other questions to ask, but the pull of the cemetery tugs on me like a magnetic force. *I need a look at those tombstones.*

An itch in my brain points out that this is strange. It's not like the tombstones are going anywhere. Then again, I don't know how long the house will keep us here. Dumping my cereal bowl in the sink, I lie to Mom without a shred of guilt. "I'm going to find Ash."

"I'm so glad you two are getting along. My plan for today is to place a few protective stones around the house, see if I can lift the mood of this place." Mom's tone suggests it'll be like bailing out a sinking boat with a sieve. I'm happy to leave her to it.

On my way, I pass Ash's dad and Linden peering through

the sliding glass door at the collapsed porch. "I'll move the wreckage," Ash's dad says. "It's a hazard."

"Is it safe?" Linden wonders. "You know what this house is like. You could cut yourself on a rusty nail and end up with tetanus."

"I've had my tetanus shots. It's a danger for the kids to leave it like this."

They catch sight of me and pause their conversation awkwardly. I pass through the door that opens into Ash's family wing, but once there, I make no move to find Ash. I locate the closest outside door and head straight for the cemetery.

The rain Windy predicted hasn't arrived, but the clouds are dark gray, the air damp and gusty. On the other side of the woods, the stone pillars of Old House lurk beneath the gloomy sky like the opening shot in a scary movie. I still have no desire to go there.

I only want to see the cemetery.

Is it weird that I don't want to invite Ash? Apprehension prickles my skin, and I touch my bear talisman for comfort. I force my feet to a halt to prove that I can. It's not like yesterday when my body wasn't my own. I can go back to the house anytime I want. There are no frogs, no nausea, no hives—nothing driving me to the one place I can never go. This isn't Carrefour magic tricking me to my doom. It's just a trip to the cemetery.

Uncle Flint's grave has been filled in. In the next row over I find the graves of the three wives who died due to improperly canned fruit in 1976. Two of them are buried beside their husbands, who followed them quickly into the ground. The third woman's grave is set aside, waiting for her husband to join her: Jasper's wife, my great-grandmother. Her name was Delilah.

Walking deeper into the rows, I find Old Linden's headstone: 1874–1976. One hundred and two years. No wonder everyone's worried about Jasper refusing to go gently into the good night, or whatever that poem says.

Old Linden is buried next to his wife, who died forty years ahead of him, and not far from his children Ruby and Rowan, who died on the same day in 1903. Each child's stone forms half a heart, with a crack between the two. The symbolism is clear: *Brokenhearted.*

The older tombstones are farther back. Thinking I might as well start at the beginning, I head for a tall monument that towers above the other headstones. My bet is it belongs to Diamon Carrefour. As I get closer, a man steps out from behind it. "Hello, Garnet."

Run! says my brain. My feet don't move.

The man pats the air the way LJ did when Oak was on the roof. Like it's supposed to calm me down. "I mean you no harm."

Do people who say *I mean you no harm* think that people who *do* mean you harm won't lie? I grab the pendant Uncle Mica gave me, calling on its power.

"Garnet," the man says. "Don't be scared. My name is David Castellano. I'm your father."

16

Rainbow Obsidian

Color: *black with iridescent colors*

Magical properties: *used for summoning*

To recharge: *place in sunlight or among crystals*

I grip the bear pendant and look the man over. His hair is dark brown, as are his eyes and his neatly trimmed beard. My eyes are a lighter shade of brown than his, and although we both have olive-toned skin, it's not an exact match. Still, he's closer to my complexion than Mom is. Plus he looks familiar. Not mirror-image familiar, but there's something about this man I recognize.

He must see the skepticism on my face, because he says, "I don't blame you for being cautious. I don't have a paternity test in my back pocket, though I do have a picture of your mother from when we were together." Reaching into his wallet, he removes a scrap of paper and places it on top of a nearby tombstone before backing away.

A breeze immediately sweeps the paper off the grave. I pick it up before it can blow away. It's a small square cropped from a larger photograph. Mom's face is caught looking toward the camera and laughing. She resembles the sixteen-year-old Emerald I met, except that her hair is swept into an updo and she's wearing makeup that makes her look older. She *would've* been older, when she met David Castellano.

Feeling wary but less afraid, I return the picture, approaching him to hand it back. He accepts the photo with fingers that seem oddly shaped. Noticing my gaze, he holds up the hand for me to see. The middle finger is shorter than the others, cut off at the first joint. My eyes widen. "Did you lose that on an archaeology dig?"

"Ha. I wish there was an interesting story. I caught my finger in a car door when I was a kid." He drops his hand. "I apologize for meeting you this way."

His apology strikes me as significant, and not just a figure of speech. Did he have something to do with getting me out here? I came to search the gravestones for deaths that happened around the same time as heir transitions. But I didn't write down any dates from the Family Book. I didn't even bring paper and pen to record what I found.

"How did you bring me here?" I demand. Magic summoned me to the cemetery. My skin prickles with anger that I succumbed so easily. Why didn't I fight harder? How dare he?

He doesn't deny it. Digging in another pocket, he pulls out a large pendant wrought in silver with an inlaid rainbow obsidian stone. "A summoning charm." He surrenders it to me. "The instructions said it was good for only one use, but I'm sure you know how to recharge it."

I glare at him before dropping my eyes to the charm. The stone whispers weakly—*Come, come, come*—but its power is mostly spent. "This is high-quality work. Where'd you get it?"

"Ordered it from an Etsy shop that is owned, I believe, by your uncle Mica."

Well, that explains why the bear amulet didn't shield me properly. Pitting two charms made by the same person against each other is risky. You never know which will prevail and what other factors, like the desire and willpower of the users, might interfere.

Stones are supposed to be my expertise, though, so I'm angry at my defenses for crumbling without a fight. I shove the amulet into my back pocket. Then, like a penny dropping through the slot of a piggy bank, I remember. I don't know if it's because I've taken possession of the amulet, breaking its hold on me, or just my magic-addled brain catching up. "You were in our shop! Over a year ago. Asking me about the difference between amulets and talismans." I scowl. "You gave me the creeps."

David—I can't think of him as my father—puts a hand over his heart. "Did I? I didn't mean to!"

It's not typical for customers to approach me with questions about magic. They say, *Can I speak to your mother?* But I was alone in the storefront that day. The clerk who works for us was on vacation, and Mom was on the computer in the back room. A man—*this* man!—came in looking for something. He seemed familiar enough with magic to make him a knowledgeable amateur, but he was content to ask me his questions, all while smiling strangely. Yes, I thought it was creepy.

"I went to get Mom to wait on you, but when we got back, you were gone."

"I was trying to avoid your mother. She's done her best to keep me from ever knowing you."

I narrow my eyes as goose bumps rise on my skin. "She told me you didn't want to be involved."

"That's not true. Your mother has done quite a lot to keep me from finding her—mundane things like registering her shop under the name Emily Carr and other, more arcane protections. Before you think the worst of her, I always believed she was trying to shield me from Jasper and the Carrefour magic, which has proved deadly to, uh, peripheral members of your family."

Think the worst of her? My mind immediately jumped the other way. *There must be a good reason Mom kept him away from us.* But I've seen the graves of the three wives who died before Old Linden passed. Maybe she was trying to protect him.

"Will you walk with me?" David asks, gesturing away from the cemetery, toward the woods. "I'd like to get to know you."

The garnet hanging against the pulse in my throat roars in warning. "I don't think I trust you enough for that." He seems legit in that he's got a photo of Mom, knows about the danger of Carrefour magic, and properly uses words like *mundane* and *arcane*. But there's something not right about this meeting—and I'm still mad about the charm that got me here.

His gaze lifts over my head. On the other side of Crossroad House, an engine chokes and rumbles. It doesn't sound like a car. "Are you not happy to meet me?"

"It's not that." Although it's kind of that. Nothing about this situation feels happy. "Why did you summon me to the cemetery?"

"Instead of ringing the doorbell? I'm not sure how Emerald would react. I understand why she sent me away. There's danger here for me, but there's also danger to you. I want to protect you during this transition."

I scowl at him. "How do you even know about that?"

"The Carrefours are a prominent family in these parts. People in town know that Jasper is sick. They say he doesn't have much time left, and *I* know what that means for the family from my days with your mom."

"How can you help us?" If Mom and her cousins are powerless, what can an outsider do?

"I have an idea of how to neutralize Jasper." Then, as if he heard the unspoken part of my question, he adds, "Sometimes it takes an outsider to see what everyone is overlooking." The roar of that strange engine grows louder, and David recoils as a tractor with a shovel lumbers around the side of the house. "Are you sure you won't take a walk with me? Just into the woods a bit...to—"

"Stay out of sight?" It's obvious David doesn't want to be seen. I glance toward the tractor. "That's Holly's husband."

"Oh, I know Simon, and he knows me. If he sees me, he'll tell your mom."

"Is that really a bad thing?"

"Do you know what Emerald, Holly, and Windy, working together, could do to me? I'd wander away from here, confused and forgetting everything it's taken me years to figure out. You'd probably never see me again. So, yes. I prefer to stay out of sight."

Rain spatters the ground. He reaches a hand toward me, and I step backward. He sighs and drops his hand. "Please don't tell anyone about meeting me. Not until I've explained my plan. Meet me back here tomorrow, around two o'clock."

"It's supposed to rain again," I say, remembering Windy's forecast.

"Bring an umbrella. For what we need to do, rain won't matter." The rain comes down harder, pinging Diamon's monument like pebbles. "I'll see you then. Together, we can beat Jasper and keep you and your mom safe!"

My feet start moving away from him, toward Crossroad House. I feel relief right away. Moving away from David Castellano is a relief, and I don't know why.

He darts toward the woods, which is a strange direction unless he's parked his car on the other side of the trees. *He's going to get drenched,* I think, but as I break into a run, I'm not quite as worried about my long-lost father as I would have expected myself to be.

17

Tourmaline

Color: *black*

Magical properties: *protects from negative energy and evil spells*

To recharge: *run water over the stone, then place in sunlight*

I pelt toward the house as the rain pelts me. The sprinkling has turned into a drumming torrent, exactly like the day Windy turned rain away from the pool.

Ash's dad has collected a scoop of broken roof and timber in the shovel of his tractor and is driving away from the house to dump it downhill. Seeing me, he raises a hand in greeting and grins ruefully, acknowledging that we've both picked a bad time to be caught outside.

Right in front of my eyes, the tractor begins to tip. I can't tell if it hit a rock, or if the ground gave way on the incline. Ash's dad reacts instantly, steering the tractor in the opposite direction for balance. But there's no stopping it. Almost in slow motion, the tractor topples downhill. He is thrown from his seat—or maybe he jumps—and disappears from sight with the tractor tumbling after him.

"Help!" I scream, looking back at the cemetery, but David has disappeared into the woods. Torn between running to the tractor and running to the house, I freeze, useless as a stick in the mud.

A side door to the house flies open, and Holly dashes out, shouting her husband's name. With Holly on the way, I skid down the slippery hill, afraid of what I'm going to find. Porch wreckage litters the slope. The tractor has landed on its side near the bottom. I don't see Ash's dad until I run around the tractor and scream. He's lying on his back with his legs underneath the machine.

His head turns in my direction, and he holds up a hand. "Don't come closer!" With agonizing slowness, he wriggles backward, easing his legs from beneath the body of the tractor. I gasp in relief. He's not pinned. But if the tractor slips...

Only when he clears the overturned machine and scrambles to his feet do I release the pent-up air in my lungs. He grabs me by the arm and pulls me away from the wreckage just as Holly runs down the hill and into his arms. "Simon!"

"It's okay! I'm not hurt." He urges both her and me up the hill.

"I told you not to take the risk!" Holly exclaims.

"You were right. I should have listened."

I shudder, wet and cold and horrified. The tractor isn't large, but if it had landed on his head or his chest, it could've killed him. Furiously, I search the second-floor windows of Crossroad House. No sign of Jasper. If he was watching *this* near disaster, he's gone now.

I go with Ash's parents back to the house, where Holly

pulls warm towels out of her dryer and hands them around. "What were you doing in the rain?" she asks me.

Now is the time to tell someone. *I met my father.* Or, more accurately, *I met someone who claims he's my father.*

I didn't feel a connection to him, but maybe that's unreasonable to expect. He had a photo of my mom when she was younger. A cropped photo. Who or what had been cut out of it? Then again, a full-sized photo wouldn't have fit in his wallet.

Toweling off my hair and delaying an answer, I consider telling Holly—who will, of course, report to Mom. If that happens, I'll have no choice in whether or not I see David Castellano again. The decision will be taken away from me.

"I was looking at the headstones in the cemetery," I finally say. "The rain started so suddenly..."

"You should stay closer to the house. And don't go anywhere near—"

"Old House. I know."

I can't tell any of the adults about my meeting today and my invitation for tomorrow. They don't even trust me to stay away from the ruins I've been warned will be my doom. But just because I can't tell *them* doesn't mean there's no one to confide in.

"You don't know if he really is your father," Ash responds immediately.

"That's why I want you to come with me tomorrow."

"Me? I'm not exactly bodyguard material. I don't think you should go."

Ash seems shaken by his dad's near miss. *I was careless. It was an accident,* his father explained. Sure. Oak's fall was an accident. So was the car wreck that killed Ash's grandparents. So was the fire that killed my grandmother. Accidents aren't really accidents when they happen at Crossroad House. Ash wasn't fooled, and now he's wary.

"What if he really does know a way to defeat Jasper?"

"Tell your mom."

"Mom lied to me about him."

"According to a guy you met in a cemetery after he used a charm on you."

I clench and unclench my hands, running through the possibilities.

A: My mother lied about my father not wanting any part of us because she was trying to protect him.

B: My mother lied about my father not wanting any part of us because my father is not a nice person.

C: My mother didn't lie because the guy in the cemetery isn't my father.

What happened to Ash's dad is a good reason to favor Option A. And the fact that Mom kept so many secrets about Crossroad House for so many years is a good reason to consider both A and B. She hides the truth when it suits her purposes.

Which is why, if I tell her about my excursion to the cemetery, she will roll me up in bubble wrap and stuff me in a closet for the duration of Jasper's transition. Then she and her cousins will do exactly what David Castellano said they'd do to get rid of him. "We'll take LJ," I decide. "We won't tell him, we'll just spring it on him at the last minute that we need his help in the cemetery."

"What makes you think he'll come?"

"Because he's LJ and we're asking for his help."

Ash exhales in exasperation. "You're right."

"Ash!" Rose shouts from the kitchen. "Pot duty! Bring Garnet!"

I grimace. Mom used to tell me that Rose was the dreamy bookworm cousin. But grown-up Rose seems angry all the time. "Are we washing pots and pans?" I ask.

"Not exactly."

Turns out, the roof leaks. What a surprise. *Pot duty* means finding the leaks and placing pots under them to catch drips. When Holly's wing is filled with a cacophony of plinks and plunks, Ash and I move to the main part of the house.

We start in the attic, where Uncle Mica has already begun laying out his rain-catching containers. Then we move to the part of the second floor that doesn't have a third story above it: the wing where Windy and her mother have their rooms. We finish up just as we run out of appropriate vessels, and we're on our way downstairs when we almost intrude on another of Rose's not-so-private phone conversations on the landline.

"—not ignoring your calls," she's saying, twirling the cord between her fingers. "My phone gets no reception here."

Ash and I stop out of her sight and start backing up.

"I really don't know," Rose answers an unheard question. "A couple of days? A week?" The distant bang of a door seems to startle her. "Hold on a second. Holly! What's wrong?"

"I can't find Oak!" Even from the other side of the house,

we hear the distress in Holly's voice. Ash and I look at each other, then clatter down the stairs.

"Gotta go." Rose slams down the phone and strides across the hall to poke her head into the front parlor, shouting, "Oak!" Turning on her heel, she disappears into the library just as Ash and I reach the first floor. We hear her shriek, "What are you doing?" and the two of us rush through the library door.

Jasper is in the chair beneath the portrait of Old Linden with Oak tucked onto his lap. Oak's tousled blond head rests on Jasper's chest, his bandaged leg hanging off the chair. If it was anyone else, in any other place, Jasper would look like a harmless, adoring great-great-uncle.

Here, the sight freezes my heart.

Rose flies at Jasper and scoops the child away from him. Oak lolls limply. He might be asleep, but Rose's face is pinched with fear.

Holly bursts into the room. She runs to take Oak from her sister's arms, screaming his name. Mom and Windy enter next, breathless as if they've been searching everywhere for the missing boy.

Ash's fingers dig into my arm while Holly tries to rouse Oak, and my mom and Windy gather around her to help. I'm opening my mouth to say something comforting—I don't know what—when Rose dives toward Jasper and slaps him across the face. The smack of flesh on flesh is remarkably loud. "You monster! Why don't you just *die*?"

There's a collective gasp from the doorway, where River, her grandmother, and LJ have appeared, drawn by the shouting. LJ waves his hands frantically, signaling Rose to control herself.

But a train couldn't have stopped Rose. "How *dare* you leech off my nephew, you disgusting old spider! We hate you! *The house* hates you! It crumbles and decays while you *take and take* what rightfully belongs to us!" She pauses for air, but those of us who are hoping she stops there are quickly disappointed. "*You* were never supposed to be the heir. Old Linden wanted Gale. My mother told me so! But you made sure Gale didn't live long enough to get the ring, and you got rid of my grandfather and Great-Aunt Hestia too. You were chosen because you were the only one left. *Give up the ring!* Anyone here would serve the family better than you!"

When Rose finally falls silent, the room darkens, as if a cloud has drifted in front of the sun. But there is no sun today, and the drapes are already closed.

Rose, you shouldn't have. Yesterday, Oak's injury terrified me. This morning, David Castellano perplexed me, and Ash's dad's accident shocked me. But none of that filled me with dread the way Jasper's face, with the red imprint of Rose's hand, does now.

Jasper puts his hands firmly on the arms of his chair and stands, bearing little resemblance to the shambling old man Holly led away from the funeral dinner. The portrait of Old Linden looms over his shoulder, as if our ancestor is standing directly behind him. I want to drag Rose away from the two of them. I want to holler, *Everybody calm down!* But under the malignant gleam of Jasper's eyes, I am frozen. A rabbit pinned by the stare of a predator.

"Anyone here could do it?" Jasper's voice is eerily calm. Rose takes a step back. "None of you know what it means to serve this family, the lengths one must go to preserve the earth magic you greedily absorb."

Shadowy corners of the library stretch their reach, consuming the bookshelves, the chairs, the tables. I wrap my fingers around my garnet amulet—and feel nothing but a cold stone against my skin.

"Not one of you understands the cost of maintaining our power over decades as the world changes around us," Jasper continues. "The bribes to the correct officials to make sure a new highway plows through *someone else's* land. Thwarting a misguided archaeology exploration that would have dug up the ley lines and disrupted their earth magic forever." His lips twist in a sneer. "Instead of learning to do what was necessary, you wasted your youth sunning by the pool and spending your inheritance in pursuit of whatever career you claimed to want, only to end up living rent-free at Crossroad House instead. One of you ran away from her responsibilities but *still* managed to live off Carrefour money."

Is that directed at Mom? What does he mean? I can't think with the buzzing in my ears, coming from everywhere and nowhere, like the house is filling with invisible bees.

"For over four decades, I have served as heir to the Carrefour power and the source of everything you hold dear." Repressed fury boils over when his eyes focus on the youngest cousin of Mom's generation. "You, Rose Carrefour, are a blind fool who *sees* nothing, *knows* nothing, and has *done* nothing to earn her place in this family. Your life channels through me. All of you have forgotten your place—which is in service to *me*." Jasper raps his cane on the floor.

Rose cries out, crumpling into a heap.

Then Holly gasps and sinks to the floor, still holding her son.

Mom and Windy are next, but they wrap their arms around Holly as they go down, bending over her, shielding Oak.

The buzzing crescendoes. The house shudders. A rancid vileness washes over me in a wave. My stomach turns to stew, swimming out my ears and streaming from my nose. The next thing I know, I'm flat on the library rug watching Jasper's magic take the people nearest the door.

LJ catches Tempest but can't stay on his feet. He slides to the floor with the elderly woman sprawled on top of him.

River, the last one standing, grimaces with the effort. She steps in front of her grandmother, her hands flickering, calling on something like the gust of wind that saved Oak. Whatever it is, she never completes the spell. Her body spins as if struck by a by a boxer. Her face collides with the doorjamb, and she drops.

The sound of our punishment, which has become a roaring, howling nightmare, grows even louder, but somehow fails to drown out a jaunty whistling.

The sound of someone feeling satisfied.

Darkness consumes the room and my eyes fall closed, but not before I see Jasper step over our bodies without the use of his cane on his way out of the library.

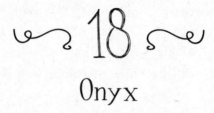

Onyx

Color: *deep black*

Magical properties: *protects from psychic attack and the evil eye*

To recharge: *apply consistent contact with wearer and other onyx stones*

The next time I pry open my eyes, I see the ceiling of LJ's bedroom. I have a memory of a rough shirt against my cheek and a bumpy ride, which may have been someone carrying me upstairs. There's also the image of Uncle Mica hovering over me. That must have been a dream since he never comes down from the attic.

But when I raise my hand to rub my gritty eyes, a cascade of bracelets slides down my arm—the two I came here with plus another I've never seen before, which I recognize as Uncle Mica's work. Does that mean he was here?

Turning my head, I see my mother beside me. She, too, is wearing a new bracelet.

Too bad the stones in the bracelets—all of them—are as silent as the rocks in the driveway. I can't hear them; I can't feel them. Their magic might be intact. They might even be effective, to a degree. But I'm as unaware of their power as any mundane, just like I was when the family magic dragged me here, barfing frogs.

My stirring wakes Mom. Her pale eyelashes flutter. "Garnet?"

"Jasper took our magic!" I wail. (Actually, it's a whimper.)

"He's blocked it," she murmurs, shifting position. "But it's not...it won't be..."

Then she's asleep again, and a moment later, so am I.

The *next* time I wake, it's to darkness behind the window, the sound of a male voice in the room, and the smell of strong tea. Opening my eyes is less of a struggle than it was before, although my ears still feel clogged by the silence of the stones.

"...Holly's blend of anise and turmeric, although I don't have her talent in the brewing," the man in the room is saying. Not Uncle Mica, then.

I roll over and blink at Mom's cousin Linden, with his precisely combed hair and his clunky, outdated glasses. He reaches across the bed with a steaming mug, which I accept. Mom is already sitting up, sipping from hers. "How is everyone?" she asks him.

"Recovering." Linden explains that the only people unafflicted were the ones not in the library when Rose confronted Jasper: Uncle Mica in the attic, Holly's husband searching for Oak outside—not that he has magic to be silenced anyway—and Linden himself, who'd been working on bank statements in the sitting room. Since the sitting room is off the main hallway, I have to wonder why Linden didn't get up to join the search for Oak.

How convenient for Jasper's favored candidate that he wasn't in the room when Jasper got really, really ticked off.

Ash's dad and Linden gathered everyone up and got them to their beds, with some help—to Linden's shock—from Uncle Mica. "After everyone was settled, Mica scoured his collection for charms and amulets and gave them to me for dispersal before planting himself in this room to watch over you while you slept."

I *didn't* imagine it. Uncle Mica came down from the attic for us!

"What has Jasper been up to, with everyone bedridden?" Mom asks.

"Walking around like a man in his mere eighties, humming to himself, making sandwiches…" Linden lowers his voice to a whisper. "It won't last. He's so riddled with cancer, magic runs through him like water in a sieve."

Mom sniffs disdainfully. That's when I remember Ash telling me that Linden voluntarily lets Jasper leech his energy from time to time, so I guess he would be the one to know. I shudder at the thought.

Linden, perhaps sensing that his welcome has run out, leaves a few seconds later.

The tea is enjoyably warm and spicy, like licorice with a bite to it. But if there's any magic in it, I can't sense it. "I hate this," I grumble.

Mom knows I'm not talking about the tea. "I know."

I finger the garnet talisman. "Uncle Mica's charm didn't work."

Mom grimaces. "Carrefour magic isn't very effective pitted against the Carrefour heir. It's not meant to work like that. But your talent will return. He's not strong enough to keep it from us as long as he'd like."

She sounds certain. "Has he done this before?"

"My brother and I went joyriding in his car when Mica was fourteen and I was twelve. We knocked down a fence and Jasper deprived us of our power for a week. But that was when he was younger. And healthy. The Carrefour magic wants to flow through all of us; it'll cost him too much to dam it up."

The Carrefour magic wants. That phrase doesn't seem strange anymore, and it reminds me of the claims Jasper threw around before he struck us down.

"Was Dav—my fa—*your boyfriend's* archaeological dig really going to interfere with earth magic?"

"That's what Jasper thought. They were excavating a suspected Stone Age site adjacent to one of the ley lines, but on our neighbor's property, so there wasn't much Jasper could do about it. At first. Then our neighbor got sick and sold Jasper the land, the dig lost its university funding, and one of the students went missing—*all around the same time.*"

"Missing," I repeat. "On the Old House property?"

Mom nods solemnly. "I told you. There've been many. The archaeology team packed up and left."

A vanished student, a sick neighbor, and Jasper gets his way. Another reason for my mother to break up with David Castellano and then vanish herself. But there was something else Jasper mentioned....

"What did he mean when he said—"

"I stole money from him." Mom doesn't wait for me to finish the question. "Ten thousand dollars in cash taken from his safe. I used it to start up the shop. It's one of the reasons I cut ties with everyone in the family. It was almost a decade before I reached out to Mica and Windy again—after I was fairly sure Jasper wasn't going to come looking for his money." Setting her mug aside, she sinks down in the bed, pressing her fingertips against her closed eyelids. "Now you know all my secrets."

But do I?

It's the perfect moment to reveal my own secrets—meeting David Castellano and the waking-dream vision of my mother and her cousins by the pool. But Mom looks so defeated right now that I want to reverse roles and protect her for a change.

If David has a real plan to defeat Jasper, I need to know what it is.

❧

My sleep is fitful throughout the night. I lie with the bracelets under my ear and keep waking myself up to check for magic. Near dawn, I finally fall into a deeper slumber and don't wake up until noon—still without magic and so queasy I can barely choke down the toast and jam Ash's dad brings. Meeting David in the graveyard today seems like an impossibility.

"Not much longer, love," Mom promises me. "Jasper can't last."

When the magic comes, finally, it doesn't trickle. It

wallops me like a wave on the beach. Think: Dorothy stepping from black-and-white into Technicolor Oz. Think: unmuting the TV and having it blast at full volume. My world tilts sideways.

My mother puts a hand to her head. "You too?"

"Yes!" I gasp.

Our bracelets hum and trill in harmony while my heart sings. My body aches like I've run a marathon, but my mind is finally clear. The first thing I do when I feel sturdy on my feet is climb to the attic to thank Uncle Mica. I hesitate when I see him, but he holds out his arms for a hug, and I run to him.

"Thank you," I say. "For watching over us."

He releases me and looks away, nodding very briefly. I know it was hard for him to leave his refuge, probably harder than I can imagine, and I'm touched that he did it anyway. But he looks embarrassed. I don't want him to feel that way. I want to protect him, the way I wanted to protect Mom, so I distract him. "What are you working on?"

Uncle Mica motions me to a sink where he's been washing and drying onyx stones. Onyx offers protection, but its power builds over time as the stone grows fond of its possessor. I'm not sure if newly acquired stones will be effective against Jasper—or if any Carrefour magic will be. Still, I help him finish the task. He puts a couple of dozen stones in a felt bag and indicates that I should distribute them among the family.

I take the bag to Mom, and we split the stones between us. "You hand them out in the main house," Mom says. "I'll take the rest to Holly's."

"Can we trade? I want to see Ash."

Crossroad House is quiet as I pass through it—the menacing presence I sensed during Jasper's tirade dormant. I see no one, although I hear the hum of gemstones in new places. Mom said she was going to plant a few wards around the house yesterday.

I find Ash and Oak in their family room, working on a jigsaw puzzle. Of the two, Oak looks more recovered. There's color in his cheeks, brightness in his eyes, and the bandage on his leg doesn't seem to bother him. Ash is wilted by comparison.

Plopping down beside them, I hand them two onyx stones each and explain what they're for. "They get stronger the more you handle them. So keep them in your pocket, and whenever you think about it, touch them." I show them the two I claimed for myself, holding them in one hand and rolling them together.

Oak presses his onyx stones against his cheeks. "Will they keep me safe from Jasper?"

Outrage stabs my heart. "They'll try," I tell him honestly.

The boy scoots toward me. "Did you know that spiders vomit acid on their victims and suck up the juicy sludge?"

I cringe. *Is that what it felt like to him, to be fed upon?* "Oak, that's awful—"

"That's what we should do to Jasper," Oak interrupts, grabbing a straw from a nearby empty glass. "Like this!" He sucks through the straw with a gleeful expression, making a disgusting noise.

"Oak!" Ash chides wearily. "Mom told you to stop saying that."

"What about what he did to Aunt Rose?"

"Aunt Rose is going to be fine." Ash rises unsteadily to his feet. "Garnet and I will give her the onyx stones. Just... stay here and work on the puzzle." He pushes me out of the room not very subtly.

I clutch the velvet bag in my hands. "I do have stones for your mom and Rose."

"Mom's resting. Earlier she dragged herself out of bed to examine Aunt Rose and to make a poultice for River." He pauses. "Her nose was broken."

Jasper slammed River against the doorjamb for daring to fight back. "I thought it might be, but what happened to Rose?"

He puts a finger to his lips to quiet me and beckons me toward the kitchen, whispering, "We hope it's not permanent."

"What?"

In the doorway of the kitchen, Ash exclaims loudly, "It's Ash, Aunt Rose! And Garnet!"

At first, I don't know why he's yelling something Rose can see for herself. Then the microwave beeps, and she pats her hand against the cabinets until she finds the microwave door handle. *Rose can't see.*

Jasper called her a blind fool, and he blinded her in punishment.

Ash rushes forward. "Let me help you with that!"

"No. I've got it." Rose removes a bowl from the micro-wave and carries it to the table. "I can see light and dark."

And not much else, I conclude when she bumps into a chair before setting the bowl down safely. As she seats herself, I notice her roots growing in—a natural strawberry blond peeking through the bright burgundy she chose to distinguish herself from her family. I'm not sure why that strikes me as even sadder than what Jasper did to her.

"If you're staring at me with pity, knock it off," Rose snaps.

Dropping my gaze guiltily, I take two onyx stones out of the bag and explain why Uncle Mica sent them. Resisting the urge to force them directly into Rose's hand, I lay them on the table and clatter them together so she can hear where they are.

She scoops them up on the first try. "Tell Mica I said thanks." She offers nothing more and begins to sloppily eat her soup. We leave, not knowing what else to say. I'm horrified by what Jasper has done, but Rose doesn't want my pity. Rose is a fighter.

Linden said magic runs through Jasper like a sieve, yet he still had the power to do this. It doesn't matter that he can't hold on to what he steals. He simply steals more.

Who will be next? What will he take?

"We missed meeting that David guy," Ash says. "You think he'll come tomorrow?"

"I hope so."

Ash yawns, his strength clearly fading. "We'll bring LJ with us and River, too. She won't let him pull any monkey business."

Bolstered by the idea of my cousins having my back, I say goodbye to Ash, who declares he's going to nap until dinner.

When I pass through the door into the main house, I smell something roasting in the oven. My stomach growl reminds me I haven't consumed anything but toast and tea since yesterday.

In spite of the tantalizing odor, there are almost forty minutes left on the oven timer. Aaargh! Grabbing a handful of cookies to keep me alive, I go looking for everyone else. I hear several people boisterously talking and laughing nearby.

Laughing? I stop in my tracks.

Very distinctly, I hear Windy's voice. "Mica, what are you doing?"

Goose bumps blossom on my arms when Mica *answers* her. "What does it look like I'm doing?"

I stare at the sliding doors in the hallway. It's dark beyond the glass—much darker than the gloom of a rain-filled afternoon. Where there should be wreckage piled against the doors, people are moving on the other side.

I hesitate, my mouth full of Oreos. Should I run and get Ash? The opportunity might vanish before I can return. Whatever the Carrefour magic wants to show me, it's on offer *now* and maybe *only* now.

Sliding the glass door open, I step back into 1998.

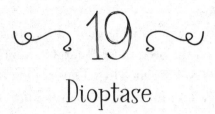

Dioptase

Color: *deep blue-green to emerald green*

Magical properties: *stimulates psychic vision and remembrance of past lives*

To recharge: *place among hematite*

The taste of Oreos vanishes from my mouth. It's night-time, and citronella candles line the porch railing, warding off mosquitoes.

My eyes—or rather the eyes of the person I am—scan the porch. Teenage Emerald sits in a glider with her feet curled beneath her. Holly is perched in a wicker chair nearby, and Windy sits in a matching one, buffing her nails.

"Any day now!" Windy sings out, glancing over her shoulder.

"The wood is wet," Mica retorts, crouching beside a fire pit just off the porch steps. "If you wanted a fire, you should have kept the firewood dry too."

Is this the same day I was here before? The evening after the afternoon rainstorm?

"Tana!" Emerald pats the seat beside her on the glider and moves her legs out of the way. "You're welcome to join us."

The girl crosses the porch and takes the offered spot. Tana is wearing a skirt tonight instead of jeans shorts, but the flip-flops are the same. Her hands—my hands—smooth the skirt nervously. Emerald propels the glider with one foot.

"Move over, dude." Brand appears out of the dark and elbows Mica. "Let a real man take care of the fire."

Mica cheerfully says something that would've gotten me in big trouble with my mother.

Teenage Emerald laughs merrily.

Brand squats beside the fire pit and shoves the wood around with a poker while Mica climbs the steps to the porch and sits against the railing. I can't get over seeing my uncle this way, young and healthy, with no idea what's ahead. Though he shouldn't be able to sense my interest inside Tana's head, his eyes shift toward me. "Did Rose ditch you again?"

"Yeah, kinda," Tana says in a pitiful tone.

"Ha!" Brand exclaims. Flames leap inside the metal fire pit. "It only took someone who knew what he was doing." He looks at Windy, seeking praise. But instead of admiring his work, Windy makes a face at Mica, who responds with a hand gesture that would have gotten me grounded but, again, makes my mother giggle.

Brand's face falls. Grabbing a folded lawn chair, he opens it with an aggravated flick of his wrist and flings himself into it, preparing to tend the fire.

"How about a spooky story?" Mica suggests.

"What are we, twelve?" Brand scoffs, then adds, "No offense, Tana."

"*I* want a spooky story." Emerald keeps the glider in motion with her foot.

"Okay then." Mica rubs his hands together, and his voice drops in pitch. "Listen up, kids. The year is 1915. A judge and a retired colonel are traveling together on a dark, rainy night when their car breaks down. Lightning illuminates the sky, and the men see two stone pillars with a metal arch stretched between them that says *Maison Carrefour.*"

Tana sits up.

"Beyond this archway, there's a house. The lights are on, so the judge and the colonel walk through the relentless, driving rain."

"But the Old Carrefour House burned in 1892," says Windy.

Mica grins. "Who's telling the story? You or me? So, its *1915,* and these stranded men walk up to the house and knock on the front door. There's no answer, but because it's raining and because the door is unlocked, they enter uninvited. Inside, the house is lit by gas lamps. Then the colonel sees something that alarms him: an open doorway, a broken serving bowl, and beside the bowl"—Mica pauses for effect—"a woman's hand."

Tana shivers, and Emerald says, "Ooooh. Go on."

Inside Tana, I'm riveted—but I also feel a sudden sense of loss. Riveted because this story must be why the house brought me here. And loss because my uncle is such a good storyteller, but in his very near future, he won't be telling any more of them.

"It's the family dining room." This younger, more confident

Mica draws the story out slowly, with long pauses between sentences ratcheting up the suspense. "The members of the household—not Carrefours, but the family that bought the property from them—had been seated for dinner. Now they're dead. Collapsed over their plates. Slumped in their chairs. Fallen to the floor."

"Poisoned?" asks Holly.

Mica raises a finger. "That's the judge's first thought. But the servants are dead too. Servants don't eat alongside their employers. They couldn't have been poisoned simultaneously. The judge, who has never seen violent death in person before, is overwhelmed. The colonel makes his way around the room, checking each person for signs of life, but the judge bolts down the hall and out the front door. He only wants a bit of fresh air..."

While the light of the fire flickers and the wicks of the candles dance, everyone holds their breath, all of us with a premonition of what's coming next.

"When he passes the threshold, the judge finds himself standing among the *ruins* of a house. It's raining, there's nothing around him but crumbled masonry, and he starts running in a panic." Mica's voice speeds up. "He dodges through a cemetery, up a long hill, and comes to another house. *This house*. He bangs on the door and collapses in the foyer when a servant lets him in."

Mica scans his audience. Windy watches him, eyes glinting with amusement. Holly shivers dramatically. Emerald has stopped rocking the glider. Brand stares into the fire as if mesmerized. As for Tana, I feel her heart thump with some emotion I can't identify.

"The servants go out to search, but there's no sign of the colonel. The owner of *this* house, Old Linden Carrefour—though not so old at the time—tells the judge that the house he claims to have entered burned to the ground in 1892. The judge falls apart completely, and police take him to a hospital." Mica pauses. "He spends six weeks in a psych ward. The colonel's family accuses the judge of killing his friend and making up the story. But with no body, there's no case. Still, for the rest of his life, the judge was suspected of having murdered his friend and inventing the story of a house that had already burned down and bodies that were two decades dead."

Silence falls over the group. That's not a satisfying ending. Tana bursts out, "Did you make this up, or is it true?"

Mica turns toward her, startled. "I don't know if the story is true, but it's true that a colonel disappeared and that his friend, a judge, gave this account to the authorities. My uncle has newspaper clippings about the incident. The public thought the judge was a murderer or possibly insane. We Carrefours, however..." Mica shrugs. "We're more open-minded."

"But I've never heard this story before," Windy declares.

"Uncle Flint says you have no patience for family history," Mica retorts.

Brand stands so suddenly he overturns the lawn chair. Tearing his eyes away from the fire, he stares at his sister. Except, right now, I'm not sure Brand is seeing his sister. There's a strange expression on his face, as if he's spotted me lurking in Tana's head. His gaze is eerie and familiar. "Tana," he growls. "Go inside."

"I don't think Mica's story scared her," Emerald objects. "Did it?"

"Not at all," Tana says, seemingly puzzled by Brand's reaction.

Brand mounts the steps to the porch. "I need to speak to you inside."

Windy looks at Emerald and rolls her eyes. I can practically see her drawing a line through Brand's name on her list of boyfriends. Brand doesn't notice. His eyes are fixed on his sister. Or me. Tana slips off the glider to meet him at the sliding glass door. Brand opens it and waves her through ahead of him.

I'm absolutely sure the first thing he'll say when we get inside is *Who are you?*

But when I step inside the house and turn around, Brand isn't there. The sliding glass door is closed, blocked by the wreckage of the collapsed porch.

I'm back in the present with no idea what that story was meant to reveal...how Tana and Brand fit into my family history, and least of all...what I'm meant to do next.

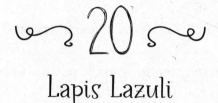

Lapis Lazuli

Color: *intense blue, sometimes mottled*

Magical properties: *enhances intuition, awareness, and understanding*

To recharge: *once a month place in a bowl of hematite*

My head is an overfilled balloon, stuffed with so many questions I don't know what to focus on.

What happened to Tana?

She has to be the girl who disappeared in 1998. Why else would the house keep bringing me back to that year and dumping me in her body? Ash said the girl vanished during the summer before the fire. How did Mom describe it? *She was staying over with us for a couple of days. She took a walk around the ruins, and no one ever saw her again.*

I assume they searched for her. There would've been police, dogs, helicopters, and probably lots of reporters. But however thorough the search and however long it lasted, Tana was never found. Just like the colonel in Uncle Mica's story.

Although, it was Uncle Flint's story first. I wish I could

ask him: *What happened at Old House in 1915? What happened in 1892?*

Since I can't, I need the help of someone who spent a lot of time with him.

⤲

"Sure," Ash says the next morning. "I know where Flint's stuff is. Sometimes he asked me to read things to him when he couldn't remember the details."

He leads me to Flint's bedroom while the adults in the house linger over breakfast, nursing their coffee and popping Advil. They don't seem to have recovered from Jasper's attack as quickly as Ash and I have.

I hang back when he opens the door, remembering that my great-uncle died in here. But the room is neat and welcoming. Ash approaches a stack of file boxes along one wall. "What'd you want to know?"

"What happened to Old House and the people who lived there."

The boxes are labeled, the handwritten letters cramped and tiny. Ash wiggles one box out of the stack so that the box above it falls into the open slot. He carries it into the center of the floor and lifts the lid.

Inside are golden, ancient newspapers, gray photocopies, and a notepad that Ash plucks from the top of the pile. "In every box, Flint kept a log summarizing the contents and his notes. We can look through the original material if you want, but the important things will be here."

"What does he say about the fire?"

Ash adjusts his glasses. "On August fourteenth, 1892,

around eight o'clock in the evening, neighbors reported a fire at the old Carrefour residence to the fire brigade marshal in town." He looks up. "Flint notes that townspeople still called it *the old Carrefour residence* even though the Carrefours had been bought out thirty years earlier. The family living there at the time was the MacArdles."

He returns his attention to the tablet. "The fire brigade went out, but there was nothing they could do. The next day, when authorities searched the ruins, they couldn't find the remains of the MacArdles. Here, Flint writes: *The authorities considered two possibilities. One, the remains were fully cremated by the heat of the flames. Two, no people were present in the house when it burned.*" Ash raises his eyes. "I'll tell you what Flint told me. The authorities believed the servants murdered the MacArdles, buried their bodies, and set fire to the house to conceal the crime."

"But that's not what happened, right?"

"There was never any proof one way or the other, although a strange thing happened in 1915—"

"A judge claimed he went into the house and saw bodies, including dead servants."

Ash's brows furrow. "Someone told you that story?"

I pause too long before saying, "Yes."

"Who?"

"I'll tell you in a minute." I can't divert the conversation.

"Okaaay." He eyes me speculatively. "So, if we believe the judge, he and his friend found the house with the family and their servants dead inside, twenty years after it burned down. And then the house disappeared again, taking the colonel with it."

"Back in 1892, after the fire, Old Linden bought back the property and built *this* house." I tap my finger against my lips. "But not on the same spot. Why didn't he rebuild on the intersection of the ley lines, where the earth magic is strongest?"

"Flint thought rebuilding on the same site might not be safe."

"Why wasn't it safe? Or—" I rephrase. "How would Old Linden have *known* it wasn't safe?"

"Good question. People vanish from there, but as far as I know, the disappearance of the colonel in 1915 was the first one. There were plenty afterward, of course. A servant in the 1930s, a hitchhiker in the 1970s, a girl who was visiting this house in 1998..."

"Tana."

Ash gives me a sharp look. "Did your mom tell you her name?"

"No. Tell me what Flint has on Tana, and I'll tell you how I know her name."

He stares at me for a few seconds, then gets up and surveys the labels on the boxes. I can tell by the way he lifts the correct one that it's light. "There's not a lot here. Flint was blinded shortly after her disappearance, and he never got more information on her. He just went over what he had, again and again."

From the top of a short stack of newspaper clippings, I pull out one with a photograph of the missing girl. It's the same face I saw reflected in the swimming pool.

Meanwhile Ash picks up a notepad. "He asked people to read the firsthand documents to him, then read him his notes, and if he thought of anything new, they'd write it down for him."

On the first page, the notes are in Uncle Flint's cramped style.

- Tana Kostopoulos, age 13 years, disappeared July 11, 1998, while visiting Crossroad House with her brother, Brand Kostopoulos, a guest of Windy Carrefour
- She was last seen by Rose Carrefour, setting off for a walk across the property
- Police searched the property, the surrounding area, and house-to-house in town, to no avail
- Dogs lost her scent at the site of Old House ruins
- The investigation was never officially closed, but physical searches ended after 2 months

The second page contains notes in the handwriting of several different people, apparently questions asked by Flint after he was blinded. Some of the questions have answers filled in.

- *How did Brand Kostopoulos meet Windy?*
  ~ Answer via Windy: At a concert.
- *Why did he bring his sister to the house?*
  ~ Answer via Windy: There were no other family members to watch her.
- *Brand was only 17. Who was Tana's legal guardian? No name appears in the newspaper articles. No guardian ever contacted the Carrefour family, nor were any lawyers or private detectives involved. WHY NOT?*
- *Where was Brand when his sister "went for a walk?"*
  ~ Answer via Emerald: At the pool with Windy and the other teens.

- *What made Tana walk to Old House?*
- *Did Rose tell the truth? ~ Answer via Rose: YES!*
  ~ But still, did she? (Uncle Flint, you need to let that
  go. Love, Emerald)

I point at the last note. "Did he suspect Rose of something?"

"I asked him that, and he said, *Rose was always hard to read.*" Ash shrugs. "It seemed like he thought Aunt Rose knew more than she let on, but she was only ten years old when Tana disappeared. She couldn't have had anything to do with it."

I'm sure Ash doesn't want to think anything bad about his aunt. But after the way Rose slapped Jasper, I'm not positive.

"So tell me," Ash says suddenly. "Whatever secret you're keeping."

How do I explain what happened to me? "If the judge and the colonel entered Old House and saw people who died twenty years earlier, do you think that was a form of time travel?"

"I hadn't thought about it that way, but—" His eyes widen in horror. "Did you—Have you been to Old House?"

"No. Not there." I heave a deep breath and plunge into the story.

It sounds unbelievable, but Ash makes no protests. He inserts a few exclamations: "Mica was talking?" and "You were in Tana's body?" When I finish, he wails, "Why didn't you tell me?" as if that was a terrible betrayal. I'm taken aback for a second. Ash and I only met a few days ago.

But we're Carrefours, and that means something.

"I was thinking about telling you after the first time, but then Oak fell through the roof. The next day, David Castellano summoned me to the graveyard, then Rose slapped Jasper and got us cursed for a day. You have to give me a pass, Ash."

He exhales in exasperation. "Okay, but show me how it works."

We leave Flint's boxes on the floor. Ash's excited expression dissolves when we get to the sliding glass door in the first-floor hallway and see only the wreckage of the collapsed porch. He grabs the door handle and tugs, but the door won't roll in its track.

"I don't think I can control when it happens," I say apologetically.

"You can't do it unless the house wants you to." He bangs a fist on the glass door. "The question is: Was it a vision, something happening only in your head? Or were you actually *there,* inside Tana Kostopoulos when she visited Crossroad House in 1998?"

I've been thinking about it as a time-traveling vision. But last time, the way Brand looked at his sister like he knew I was inside her head...How creepy would it be if my consciousness was present at Crossroad House before I was born?

"*Why* is another good question," I add. "*Why* did the house show me these events?"

"It would help if we knew more about Tana."

There's no avoiding it. We have to talk to Rose.

21

Obsidian

Color: *deep black or dark green*

Magical properties: *protects against attacks, reveals half-truths*

To recharge: *place in sunlight*

"Why do you want to know about Tana?" Rose asks irritably.

We found her in Holly's kitchen, creating a blend of tea with her sister's herbs. She seems to be able to identify each substance by smell or the taste of a tiny dab on her fingertip.

"I've been telling Garnet about the house's history," Ash explains. "She's interested in what happened to Tana, but I don't know much about her."

"You haven't been to the ruins, have you? You're absolutely forbidden."

"We haven't been to the ruins," Ash says, in the tone of someone who's promised the same thing many times. "We're just curious about Tana, and you're the person who knew her best."

"I don't know why you think that. I hardly knew her at

all." Rose slaps an aluminum jar of dried sassafras on the table, then sighs. "Sorry. When I was a kid, I resented questions about Tana. I thought everyone blamed me for losing her. The fact is, they brought her here and shoved her at me, like I should be grateful to have a playmate. But she was three years older than I was. She didn't want to play with me, or watch TV with me, or have anything to do with me."

"What *did* she want to do?" I ask. "Hang out with the older kids?"

"No. She poked around the house, getting into stuff. Sometimes I'd catch her staring at a candle flame like she was mesmerized. She asked nosy questions about our family. I found her once with the Family Book and told her she wasn't allowed to touch it." Rose snorts. "That ticked her off. Honestly, Tana was weird."

Ash adjusts his glasses nervously. "Um, don't get mad, Aunt Rose, but Flint always thought there was something you knew about Tana and didn't tell anyone. There *wasn't*, right?"

To my surprise, Rose says, "There was something else. I told Jasper, and he told me not to tell anyone. Ever. And I never did because I was afraid of him." She flips her burgundy hair over her shoulder. "Well, I'm done being afraid. You can take out a front-page ad, for all I care, that says Tana went to the ruins because she could *see* Old House. She asked me about the house she sometimes saw from the third-floor window."

Ash leans forward, his eyes wide. "She could see it?"

"Sometimes. That's the way she put it. *The house I sometimes see.*"

Ash and I look at each other. "Tana saw Old House before she disappeared," I repeat.

"Just like the colonel saw the house before *he* disappeared," Ash states.

Rose leans across the table, her unfocused eyes aimed in our direction. "I don't know who the colonel was, but if either of you ever see Old House...run as fast as you can in the opposite direction."

✍

At lunchtime, a thunderstorm rolls in. The lights flicker ominously, and Crossroad House groans.

If this lasts all afternoon, it'll ruin any chance of meeting David Castellano in the cemetery. I enjoy a brief flurry of hope when Windy and River don raincoats and walk out into the storm. But, to my disappointment, they tramp around the perimeter of the house and return, rumpled and windblown, while the storm rages on.

"The house is protected," Windy announces to Linden, tossing back her hood. Behind her, River does the same, and I stifle a gasp at her swollen nose and the blue-black bruises under both her eyes.

Linden raises his eyebrows questioningly as a gust of wind tries to pick up the house and toss it around like a Monopoly hotel.

"The house is protected from lightning," Windy clarifies. "And we created a barrier to direct rain away from the foundation wall at the top of the driveway. It'll hold. For now." Her green eyes pass over to me, where I'm shamelessly eavesdropping from the front stairs. "Pot duty will go on as scheduled, I'm afraid."

Taking the hint, I schlep off to check the pots, starting

at the back of the second floor before heading up to the attic. Uncle Mica empties his own pots when they get full, but I dump out the half-full ones in the attic apartment shower just to be helpful. Then I gaze out the large picture window facing the cemetery and the woods. Nothing out there but heavy skies and patches of flooded ground.

No shadowed figure lurking behind a headstone.

No miraculously reconstructed Old House looming amid the trees.

Something touches my shoulder, and I stifle a shriek. Uncle Mica jumps back and withdraws his hand. He looks at me questioningly and makes an *Okay?* sign.

"Yeah. I'm okay. Everything just looks extra creepy today."

I immediately regret using the word *creepy* to describe his home, but he rolls his eyes as if to say *Tell me about it.* Removing a pair of onyx stones from his pocket, he clacks them together and raises his eyebrows at me.

"Yes, I have them." I produce my own and roll them between my fingers. They hum softly, making a small chorus with the pair in my uncle's hand. His are louder because he's owned them longer, but mine are coming along. Beneath their hard, smooth surfaces, they vibrate, as if populated with tiny bees. It feels nice, although I no longer have any confidence that stones work against Jasper, a stone worker himself.

Saying goodbye to Uncle Mica, I head down to Uncle Flint's bedroom, where Ash is digging through documents. Over the next two hours, while rain pummels the windows, we read everything inside the Old House box: newspapers, letters, postcards, and even greeting cards with long messages written inside. But we don't find a single mention of anyone seeing Old House after it burned down—except for the two men in 1915.

That night Mom and I go to bed early, and I fall asleep to the angry noise of the storm and conflicting notions. The truth about Old House is either lost in Uncle Flint's files—or nowhere. David Castellano is biding his time to meet with me—or was discovered by Mom and sent away with a few strong spells. At some point long after midnight, I startle awake...

...and find myself walking along the second-floor hallway of Crossroad House.

I'm fairly sure this isn't a dream, although I have no memory of getting out of bed. The swish of fabric around my legs and the smell of the flame I'm holding in front of me are too vivid for me to be asleep. I'm definitely not in my own time, but this isn't 1998 again unless Tana was prone to carrying an oil lantern around in the dark.

My (someone's) hand reaches out to turn the knob of the door leading to the attic, and the ivory skin tone reaffirms that this is not Tana Kostopoulos. So does the long ruffled skirt that the girl lifts away from her feet as she (we) climb the stairs.

I'm confused. I mean, more than usual. I don't understand the mechanism for these time-traveling visions, but I assumed they were triggered by walking through that sliding glass door downstairs because that's where they always happened. And I get, sort of, why the house took me to see my mother and her family as teens. It wanted to tell me about Tana and Old House. But why am I climbing the stairs to the third floor in the middle of the night with some random person from the time before electricity?

The attic is not a workshop, but a schoolroom. Moonlight illuminates bookshelves, a globe on a stand, two desks with benches, and a freestanding chalkboard. Written on the board in precise chalk print:

A is for Aquamarine
B is for Beryl
C is for Carnelian
D is for Diamond

A weird way to teach the ABCs, though not in a Carrefour home.

The painted drywall that set apart Uncle Mica's apartment is missing. In its place are wooden walls separating a much smaller space. A closet, maybe?

Heels click on the wooden floorboards as this girl crosses the room, heading for the old nursery. Before she can reach it, the door opens a few inches, revealing a child wearing a dressing gown over a nightdress and slippers. "Who's there?" the little girl whispers.

The person with the lantern speaks. "Hello, Ruby."

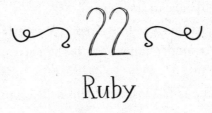

Ruby

Color: *pink or purple to deep red*

Magical properties: *promotes lucid dreaming, clarity, and wisdom*

To recharge: *run water over the stone twice a month, keep away from sunlight*

Ruby Carrefour pushes the nursery door open wider. Ruby Carrefour, who died in 1903 at the age of five.

She looks a lot like she does in the portrait, although her brown hair is tied up in strips of cloth all over her head. Rag curls, I realize. In the morning, when the strips are removed, her hair will fall into ringlets. "Who are you?" Ruby asks, unafraid but curious.

"I'm a visitor," the other girl says. Her voice sounds young, probably close to my age. "Did I wake you?"

"No. Miss Grundle went to bed early with a head-ache, but we were still playing." The child looks toward what I thought was a closet, and I realize it's just big enough to contain a bed for whoever wrote that lesson on the chalkboard. "Would you like to come in?" Ruby asks politely. "We'll have to stay quiet."

My host brushes her free hand against her frilly skirt, wiping away a sudden dampness. Is she nervous? "I would like that very much."

Ruby beckons her visitor. "This will be fun. We have lots of toys."

I don't expect the nursery to look like the grimy storage room I saw earlier today, but I always imagined it would be a depressing place. Instead, gas wall lamps cast a warm glow over a room bursting with color. Matching curtains and rug feature scarlet flowers and green ribbons against a cream background. The wallpaper alternates textured creamy stripes with a scarlet fleur-de-lis pattern. Two beds tucked into the corner of the room are heaped high with blankets and pillows.

The visitor's eyes pass over all this quickly, landing on the other half of the "we" Ruby mentioned: a small boy dressed for bedtime squatting on the rug among rows of tin soldiers. He looks up with dark eyes under brown hair cut in bangs long enough to skim his eyebrows. My host's heart thumps in response.

"This is my brother, Rowan," Ruby says in a dignified manner, like a tiny adult introducing royalty. "Rowan, please welcome our guest..." Suddenly, she looks embarrassed. "You didn't tell me your name."

The visitor turns down the flame in her lantern and sets it on a small table covered with red cloth. "My name is a secret. In fact, my visit has to remain a secret. You mustn't tell anyone I was here."

To me, this screams *Stranger Danger!* Ruby clasps her hands together in delight and Rowan bounces on his toes. "A secret!" Rowan repeats with the barest hint of a lisp.

Ruby grins. "I am very good at secrets!"

"An important skill," the visitor points out with apparent seriousness.

"What would you like to play tonight?" Ruby asks, gesturing around the room.

"Soldiers," Rowan promptly replies.

"Rowan, I was asking our guest!"

The visitor looks around the room again, slower this time. There's a rocking horse, a knee-high model sailboat, and a dollhouse. Marionettes hang from pegs on the wall, and train tracks skirt the perimeter of the room. There are china dolls and doll carriages, stuffed animals, and wooden tops. A kite hangs from the ceiling. "You do have a lot of toys."

"Papa buys us anything we ask for," Ruby says matter-of-factly.

"How nice of him." There's a hint of sadness in her voice and the edge of a sharper, harsher emotion. "You pick what we play."

Rowan's mouth opens, no doubt to suggest soldiers again, but Ruby speaks first. "Let's play with my colors. They're new!" From a pocket in her dressing gown, Ruby produces a box of Crayola Crayons.

If I'd been in control of my own lungs, I would have gasped in surprise. They had crayons back then? The design on the box is old-fashioned, but it's an eight-pack, the same eight colors you can get in any store today.

The visitor seems less surprised. "That sounds like a good idea."

Ruby opens a large pad of drawing paper and places it on the center rug. She and Rowan settle around it, and the visitor sinks down beside them, tucking her legs under her skirt. Ruby sets about coloring a field of flowers and rather bossily instructs her visitor to draw a rainbow. Rowan observes without participating—sulking, I assume, until he declares, "Rainbows come after storms!" Picking up the black crayon, he scribbles thunderclouds. "Growl, boom, bang."

The visitor, I notice, pays more attention to the children than her artwork. She studies them while their heads are bent toward the paper as if memorizing their features. Her vision grows watery. When she dashes away tears, Ruby catches her. "Why are you sad?" the child asks.

"I just have something in my eye."

She's lying. She *is* sad. Heck, *I'm* sad. It was bad enough when they were only names on gravestones. Now I've met them! The thing is, *I* know these adorable, charming children are going to die, but how does she?

I sense her grief and, more than that, her anger. I heard it in her voice earlier and now I feel it in the way her right hand clenches the crayon.

Who is this girl? Why is she visiting the Carrefour children in the night, secretly, without telling them her name? How does she know their fate? And how did she even get into the house?

More importantly, why am *I* here? The other visions the house sent me felt purposeful. So why here, now, *this*?

It's morbid, spending time with these doomed children, and I wish I had my garnet pendant for comfort.

The nameless visitor asks about their day. Ruby cheerfully lists her activities: first there were school lessons with Miss Grundle, then music lessons with Mama, and finally magic lessons with Papa.

The visitor perks up. "What magic is your papa teaching you?"

"Deafen words," says Rowan.

"Defense wards," Ruby corrects him primly. "For protection against bad spells."

"Hmm." That seems meaningful to the visitor. "I trust you study hard?"

"Papa says I have an affin-ty for it," Ruby declares. Inwardly, I smile because her pronunciation is not as advanced over Rowan's as she thinks it is.

At this point, Rowan yawns so widely, his jaw creaks.

"Silly me, I'm keeping you up." The visitor collects the crayons and puts them back into their box.

"I'm not tired." But Ruby has to smother her own yawn.

"You have lessons tomorrow and wards to learn."

"With Miss Grundle asleep, I suppose there's not anyone to tuck us in tonight." Both children look hopefully at their visitor, who smiles and says that of course she'll do it.

I watch, a passive observer, while this girl tenderly bundles both children into their sumptuous beds in their gorgeous nursery filled to the brim with toys. "Will you come again and play soldiers?" Rowan asks sleepily.

"I will try." She kisses each of them on the top of

their heads, then moves around the room turning off the gas lamps one by one. When the light from the last one is extinguished, the room plunges into greater darkness than I was expecting. I lose my balance, flail my arms, and strike something, which falls to the floor with a thud.

Belatedly, I understand that I have control over my body again.

Lightning flickers outside, briefly brightening the room. Gone are the drapes, the rug, the beds, the children, and the toys. The wallpaper is so gray, I can hardly see the fleur-de-lis pattern. There's nothing in this room except what was put here for storage long ago and the pots that I brought up myself.

At my feet is the object I knocked off a stack of boxes: an old shoe box filled with envelopes. I pick up the spilled items and find myself holding a photograph of teenage Emerald, Windy, and Holly in their bathing suits. It looks identical to the one hanging on the wall back home, in our apartment above the shop.

I don't believe in coincidence. Not in this house.

It's too dark to examine the photos by random flashes of lightning, and I don't want to wake Uncle Mica by turning on lights. So I make my way through the old nursery room, across Uncle Mica's workshop, and down the stairs to the second floor. Cringing at every floorboard creak—which only happens in the silent moments between thunder, thanks very much, Crossroad House—I tiptoe into Uncle Flint's room, close the door, and flip the light switch.

The envelopes of photographs are labeled with the name of the person who ordered them: *Opal Carrefour.* My grandmother. Some of the envelopes are older than 1998, but the one with the picture of my mom and her cousins at the pool is dated July 10, 1998—the day before Tana went missing.

There are two more photos of the girls in their swimsuits, and now that I look closer, they aren't identical. Each one is different, and one is out of focus. Back then, you couldn't choose your best photos and delete the rest. You had to get the whole roll of film developed and see what you ended up with. Maybe that's why Grandmother Opal—or whoever wielded the camera—took multiple pictures of the same thing.

I find three shots of ten-year-old Rose with her natural strawberry-blond hair, reading a book in a hammock. She looks cranky. There are two shots of Windy's mother gardening in a straw hat, and then...

I examine the next two pictures carefully. Someone photographed Brand and Tana by the goldfish pond. Tana's pose looks just like the photo in Uncle Flint's newspaper clipping. Grandmother Opal must have given a picture from this set to the newspapers after her disappearance. The ones left behind are similar, except that in the second one, Brand is holding bunny ears behind his sister's head.

The hair on the back of my neck stands on end.

Brand's second finger, the middle finger, ends at the first joint.

23

Larimar

Color: *various blues, sometimes streaked with white or red spots*

Magical properties: *opens the mind to new ways of thinking*

To recharge: *place in strong sunlight*

The man I met in the cemetery—who called himself David Castellano and claimed he was my father—is Brand Kostopoulos, brother of the missing girl. Fury flashes through me. *He tricked me!*

Followed, a moment later, by another thought: *Actually, he didn't. I never fell for his story. Not all of it.*

I had sensed something wrong about him. He was awkward, stilted, *rehearsed*. He talked too quickly, like he was anxious to feed me information that would get me to...what?

Will you walk with me? he asked. And my garnet pendant roared in warning.

More than once, he asked me to leave the cemetery and walk with him in the woods adjacent to the Old House ruins. Was he trying to trick me into going to the one place I'm forbidden to go? *Why?* Some kind of sick revenge?

Flipping through the rest of the photos, I find snapshots of my mother and her cousins doing the kinds of things teenagers do: swim, sunbathe, goof around. I come across a few of my mom with her hair pinned up, like in the photo David/Brand showed me. He's in the picture too, with his arm around Windy—which is why he cropped it.

I stuff the photos back in the envelope. So, Brand Kostopoulos tracked down Mom's shop to talk to me. Why? Does he blame Mom for inviting Tana to sit with them the night Uncle Mica told a spooky story about Old House?

But Tana was already interested in Old House before Uncle Mica's story, according to Rose. She could *see* it.

Sometimes.

Turning off the light in Uncle Flint's room, I return to LJ's bedroom, where Mom still sleeps, oblivious to my early-twentieth-century nighttime excursion. My head is heavy from exhaustion. I feel like I've been trying to pick one thread out of a tangled mess, the one that will unravel the knots and release the right answers. *But I'm missing a crucial piece of information.* In the morning, I'll have to tell Mom everything and hope that she's the one with the loose thread.

And that she won't be completely furious I didn't tell her sooner.

(Fat chance of that.)

❧

Morning comes early and abruptly with sharp knocking on the bedroom door. I groan and consider hiding under my pillow. Mom sits up. The door is thrust open before she can answer it. "Em," Windy says without apology for the intrusion. "My mother's not well. I sent River to fetch Holly. Will you come too?"

Mom doesn't waste time answering. She pulls on yoga pants under her sleep tee and dashes out of the room.

Sleepily, I get dressed and follow voices to the other second-floor hallway. In one of the bedrooms, Windy, Mom, and Holly are discussing the best treatment to raise the ailing woman's blood pressure. When Holly runs out to fetch one of her special brews and nearly knocks me down, I retreat. The most helpful thing I can do is stay out of their way.

Telling Mom about Brand will have to wait.

So, back to bed? Or downstairs to breakfast?

Breakfast, of course.

As I pass Jasper's open bedroom door on my way to the main staircase, he calls out. "Garnet!"

I pause, debating the pros and cons of responding. I'm not in his line of sight, but he speaks again as if he knows I'm still in earshot. "What were you doing in the old nursery last night?"

I walk back to Jasper's doorway. "How'd you know I was up there?"

Jasper has the largest bedroom in the house. It's clean and well lit, but decorated in a way that was fashionable in the 1960s. Jasper is seated in a chair near one of the windows. "I hear when someone's on the stairs." He indicates the wall separating his bedroom from the attic steps.

I haven't seen Jasper since the incident in the library, and I'm shocked by how much frailer he looks. Gone is the towering man who struck us all down. This Jasper hunches, his shoulders bowed and his head hanging between them. His bony hands clutch the edge of a crocheted blanket draped over his lap as if clinging to its warmth, reminding me of what Linden said: *Magic runs through him like water in a sieve.*

"How'd you know it was me?" I ask.

His stolen power might be gone, but his eyes are keen and alert. "I know the members of my family when they move about my house. By their magic."

The adjacent door in the hallway slams open and footsteps pound up the stairs to the attic. Jasper's bedroom wall actually vibrates. "And by their footsteps," he sighs. "That's Emerald. Always in a hurry, your mother."

She's probably fetching gems from Uncle Mica's workshop to help Windy's mother. Jasper probably knows his niece is sick, but in case he doesn't, I don't want to be the one to tell him another Carrefour might be dying to give him a few extra days.

Jasper waves a trembling hand. "Sit with me. Spare your great-grandfather a moment of your company."

Pride nips at me, even though I'm supposed to stay away from him. *I'm not afraid of you, Jasper.* Spying a narrow chair, I drag it into a position that puts me on the opposite side of the room with the bed between us. His wry smile suggests my maneuver is not lost on him.

"You have questions," he says, eyeing me closely.

So. Many. Questions. "What happened to Old House? Why does it suck people out of existence?"

His eyebrows waggle and lurch, but only a second passes before he answers. "My grandfather Linden cast a spell that did not go the way he planned."

I didn't expect such an honest reply. "Do you *know* this, or is it just your theory?"

"He didn't tell me, if that's what you mean. But it's

obvious. Once the MacArdle family vanished, Linden could buy back the property—but with the house burned, he had to build a new one half a mile from the intersection of ley lines. I know he was not happy about that."

A shiver of unease passes over me. "So it was him. He caused...whatever happened to Old House. But where did he go wrong?"

My mother's footsteps rattle the wall again, marking her passage down from the attic with whatever she and Uncle Mica selected. Jasper smiles wanly. "What do you think your mother is willing to sacrifice to bring Tempest back to good health?"

What a strange question! "She'll use every bit of magic she has, trying to help."

"*Every bit* of magic?" Jasper repeats doubtfully. "Would she sacrifice her magic itself, if that's what it took? What makes a sacrifice, Garnet? It's not really a sacrifice unless it's something important, is it?"

"Why does she have to sacrifice anything to make someone well?" That's not the way Mom and I do magic. What he's suggesting sounds profane.

"She doesn't have to," Jasper agrees. "Our magic doesn't require a sacrifice unless you ask for something very, very big. Which my grandfather did. He made a sacrifice, and he had to live with the results."

This conversation is making me uncomfortable. "What do you think happened to Tana Kostopoulos?" I blurt out, shifting the subject.

"She got caught in the remnants of the miscast spell because she went where she'd been told not to go."

"*Was* she told? She heard a story about Old House from

Uncle Mica, but he never told her not to go there. No one else knew about that story—at least, Mom and Windy and Holly didn't. Did *any* of them know how dangerous Old House was before Tana disappeared?"

Jasper leans forward. "How do you know what was said to the girl and what the family knew or didn't know at the time?"

Oops.

I'm tempted to lie, but he's watching me with such intensity, I get the uncanny feeling he already knows. What if he's the Carrefour with the crucial piece of information that unravels this mystery? Now that I think about it, isn't he the most likely candidate? "I know because I was there. I was in Tana's head for several minutes while she was here at the house."

"Well, well, well. What a surprise." But his expression is one of vindication, not surprise. He sits back in his chair. "That's why you were in the old nursery last night, isn't it? Moving to Crossroad House has coaxed a latent talent out of you. And I thought that particular ability had died out of the family line."

"It's a family talent?" Now I'm the one on the edge of my seat.

"An individual gift, separate from the skill we have for one earth element over another. Like Windy's divination."

"And mine is called?"

His gnarled hand points at the table beside his bed. "Open that drawer. Look for a photograph in a cardboard frame."

I do as I'm told, rummaging through empty prescription bottles and coins and broken watches before finding a small cardboard folder.

Inside is a sepia-colored photograph of a girl about River's age. She has wavy hair pulled back from her forehead by a horizontal white headband, like a flapper. Her gaze challenges the camera with intelligent eyes and a mischievous smile.

"That's my mother," Jasper says. I do a double take, look at the girl again, then at Jasper. "You're thinking my father must have been very ugly and I took after him."

"I wasn't!" (I was.) "There's a painting of her downstairs in the library. You're in it, and she—" I see it now, the resemblance between this girl and the woman in that painting. The eyes, the mouth—the spirit. This is Stella Carrefour, sister of Ruby and Rowan and the only one of Old Linden's children to survive childhood.

"My mother was a time-walker," Jasper says. "Today they'd probably give it a pseudoscientific name, like temporal bilocation. It was a rare talent, and by the time of your mother's generation, completely forgotten."

"Time-walker," I whisper, gazing at the hundred-year-old photograph.

"Some visited the past only in their minds, as you did, inhabiting the body of a different person. My mother was a full time-walker, with the ability to move her own body through the past."

The realization hits me with enough shock that I might as well have stuck a fork in an electric socket. It was *Stella* who visited Ruby and Rowan. Of course she wouldn't give her name! How could she explain being their baby sister, growing into a young woman after their deaths, and time-walking to visit them? How sad it was, and also how wondrous, that she was able to meet them at all.

Jasper is still speaking. "You asked if I know for certain what my grandfather did at Old House. The truth is I believe my mother knew, from personal observation, but she would not speak of it. She rarely spoke *to him,* either, which was how I knew she was angry about what he'd done."

"She was the last Carrefour with this talent before me?"

"Yes. Hestia—my sister—claimed to have visions through the veil of time, but it was simple divination, in my opinion."

Until this moment, I was swept up in these unexpected confidences from Jasper, but the mention of Hestia reminds me of the things he's suspected of—murdering his brothers and scaring off (or secretly killing) his sister. That talk of sacrifice…Was he referencing Old Linden, or admitting to Oak's accident, the near miss for Ash's dad, and Windy's mother's illness?

I close the cardboard folder on Stella's photograph and start to put it back in his drawer. Then, on second thought, I prop it on top of the nightstand, angling it so Jasper can't escape Stella's gaze. If she was angry with her father for whatever he did, I don't think she'd like how her son's rivals for the family power met tragic, mysterious ends.

"Garnet?" River sticks her bruised face into the room. "Phone for you downstairs. It's Oak."

Oak? "Why is Oak calling me on the house phone?"

"How would I know? I didn't stop to chat. Mom and Grandmother need me." River shoots Jasper a look of resentment and withdraws.

It's strange that Oak would call me, but Jasper has started spilling family secrets. I don't want to leave now to answer the phone. "I'll call him back," I say.

But Jasper has turned his face away from me, his head cocked as if he's listening to something I can't hear. Or sensing something I have no capacity to perceive. One corner of his mouth curls, and it gives me the creeps. "No, you can go now."

"But—"

"I'm tired," he announces, looking back at me.

He's not tired. He wants me to leave for some reason, and I don't like the chill that runs down my back at the half smile on his face. I'm out of the chair and his room in a flash.

It takes me five seconds to reach the bottom of the staircase, where River has left the old-fashioned phone receiver lying on its side. I pick it up. "Hello?"

"Garnet?" Oak's voice sounds far away.

"Hi, Oak. What's up?" I'm only half paying attention, my eyes wandering up to the second floor in the direction of Jasper's room. What happened just now? It was like Jasper received some silent message. From the house?

"You have to come to the cemetery."

My brain boomerangs back to the phone in my hand. "What did you say?"

The connection crackles. "You have to come to the cemetery," Oak repeats.

"Are you calling from the house?"

"No. Hurry," the boy whimpers. "And…he says… come alone."

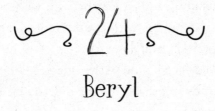

Beryl

Color: *pure beryl is colorless, but the stone is often tinted by impurities*

Magical properties: *serves in divination, images may forewarn and solve problems*

To recharge: *cleanse in fire*

I burst out of the house at a dead run. If I thought I was furious last night, it's nothing compared to now.

How *dare* he frighten Oak!

I'm not afraid of Brand. He's a poser, one of teenage Windy's cast-off boyfriends with some kind of bizarre revenge plan targeting my family through me and my mother. Whatever he's up to now with Oak, he's not going to get away with it.

The rain has stopped, but the sky is overcast and the grass slick. My sneakers slap the ground, spattering my jeans as I run. The stone wall around the cemetery partially blocks my view, but what I see seems deserted. When I reach the gate, I don't spot anyone inside at first. Then I turn to the left and discover not only Oak, but also Ash, sitting on the ground with their backs against the wall. "David Castellano" squats nearby, although now I recognize Brand Kostopoulos with twenty more years, probably thirty more pounds, and a beard.

Oak is red-faced, and Ash's glasses look broken. I clench my hands into fists. "What did you do to them?" I demand of Brand.

"Get down," he says gruffly.

"I know who you really are!"

"I said, get down!" This time he moves his hand so I can see the gun.

The feeling runs out of my extremities. Clutching my bear pendant, which roars wildly, I sink to a crouch. I have never seen a gun in real life before. Onyx stones and garnet charms can't protect me from bullets. It was stupid for me to come out here without telling anyone, to confront a man who already lied to me. Just because he was once an awkward teenager doesn't mean he's not dangerous now.

Brand waves me closer, and I scuttle over to the wall. My arms and legs move clumsily, like they aren't properly attached. *He's got us crouched behind the wall so we can't be seen from the house.* He doesn't know it isn't necessary. Half the family's attention is fixed on a sick woman. Rose is blind, Uncle Mica's a hermit, and Ash's dad fetches groceries from town every morning. Who's left? LJ and his dad? They have no reason to gaze out the window at the cemetery.

Nobody will be looking for us. No one will even notice we're gone.

"Garnet," says the man with the gun, "this is going to be a shock to you…"

"You're Brand Kostopoulos," I blurt out.

He freezes, then continues in a colder tone, "Or maybe it won't. Regardless, this is your fault. If you'd met me here when you promised, these two would never have been involved."

"He's been camping in the woods," Ash says to me.

"The boy was skulking around my tent this morning. What was I supposed to do?" Brand looks aggrieved, like he was tricked into taking Ash captive. "Then the other one showed up looking for him." He throws up both hands. "Just as well, I suppose. The older boy refused to speak on my phone even after I finally got enough service to connect."

I flinch at the gun being waved around carelessly. "Please. Let us go."

"I can't. Not until this is over."

That sounds ominous. I lick my lips. "I know you want revenge for your sister."

"Revenge?" he repeats. "What good would that do me? I want my sister back."

Ash and I exchange a quick glance. Brand is crazy.

He waves the gun again. "Out the other gate. All three of you." He glances worriedly toward Crossroad House. "Give me no trouble, and I won't hurt you."

Ash stands cautiously. "I promise I won't give you any trouble if you leave Oak here."

"He'll run for help, and I'm not going to chance anyone trying to stop me. *Move.*"

We make our way through the rows of tombstones, in the direction Brand points—toward the far gate, the *old* gate, the one closest to the ruins of Old House.

"Why'd you say you were my father?" I ask.

"I thought it would make you trust me. I've waited years for this, and I didn't want to blow it." He gestures with the gun for us to keep moving.

I wish he'd stop doing that. "*What* have you been waiting for?"

"For you to be the right age."

"You're not making sense!"

But he talks over top of me, almost babbling. "I first saw you on the night before Tana vanished. You were on the porch with us, clinging to Tana like a hitchhiker. Time-walking. Exactly the way my mother described it."

He did see me! I gape at him, still lacking some crucial piece of information. He herds us through the trees that lie between the cemetery and the ruins. "I had no idea who you were at the time. It wasn't until I had later visions—you with Emerald—that I figured out who you were. Or, rather, who you were going to be."

Suddenly Ash blurts out, "Why were you camping in the woods in the rain? Why didn't you stay in town?"

Because he's a crazy psychopath. Duh.

But Brand glances at Ash with grudging respect. "Because the woods is the farthest I can get from the house. I've been living on protein bars and instant coffee for days."

I don't understand until Ash states it outright. "You're stuck on this property like we are. You're a Carrefour."

"Smart kid," Brand grunts. "Your mother and her cousins never suspected it, no matter how many hints I gave them."

Oak looks bewildered by this stranger claiming to be a Carrefour, but I'm immediately skeeved out. "You dated Windy!" I protest.

He makes an aggravated sound. "It wasn't serious."

Ash's mind is on more recent events. "It was you who broke into the house the night before Flint's funeral. You put your blood in the Family Book."

"It was a compulsion. I was almost sick to death. It was all I could do not to write my name in its proper place and give myself away, but the blood ended up being enough." By now we've entered the woods, and as the trees obscure our view of Crossroad House, the chance of anyone there spotting us diminishes.

"What *is* your proper place?" I ask. Branches overhead drip cold water on our heads.

"He's gotta be Hestia's grandson," Ash says, taking Oak's hand when his brother slips on the leaves.

"Her son," Brand corrects him. "She was a lot younger than her brothers, and she had me and Tana late in life. A whole generation got skipped in our branch of the family."

"Hestia's earth element was fire. Which means what? Summoning fire, controlling fire..." Ash scowls. "The fire that killed Garnet's grandmom—was that you?"

"No! What kind of monster do you think I am?"

We all look at his gun.

Brand pales and shoves the weapon into his back pocket. I cringe, expecting it to go off, but it doesn't. "I swear, I had nothing to do with that fire. If I'd been here when it happened, I might've been able to stop it. But I was long gone by then. Tana had vanished and my only chance of saving her was years away." His eyes fall on me.

The Old House gateposts appear through the trees, close enough that goose bumps rise on my arms. "I still don't have any idea what you're talking about," I say impatiently.

"Having visions is part of fire magic." Brand grabs me and Oak, hustling us forward. "Tana and I never exhibited that ability until we came here. Proximity to the ley lines triggered it, but we weren't experienced enough to understand what we were seeing. I barely figured out what was going on when I saw you that night on the porch.

"After Tana disappeared, I saw you over and over. But I had no idea who you were until I had a vision of you and Em together in a gem shop and realized you were her daughter. Problem was, Em didn't have a daughter—wasn't even old enough to have a daughter your age. That's when I realized I was going to have to wait years for you to show up."

The stone pillars that once framed the gateway to Old House loom over us. The prickles I've been feeling on my arms crawl up my back and onto my scalp. Despite Brand's grip, I dig in my heels. Oak goes limp and sags to the ground.

"Yeah, I know you don't want to get closer." Brand lets go of Oak but drags me forward. "There's a repellent spell on this place, probably placed by Old Linden and renewed now and then by Jasper. They knew this place was a Venus flytrap for life energy and didn't want family wandering in by accident. Windy and Em and that whole group were clueless about what happened here. The spell dampened their curiosity, so they had no interest in exploring the ruins."

"Then why didn't it work on Tana?" I ask.

"Her visions must've been stronger than the spell." His eyes soften as he gazes through the skeletal remains of the gate, before snapping back to attention. "You can ask her when you meet her."

He's insane. Tana's been gone over twenty years.

"Don't make her go in there!" Ash barrels full tilt at our captor, butting his head into Brand's belly. It doesn't go the way Ash probably planned. Brand makes an *oof* sound. Ash bounces off his torso and lands on his rear end in sodden leaves and mud.

"Really, kid?" Brand pulls the gun out. Oak, left behind a few yards ago, poises to run back to Crossroad House, but Brand swings the weapon in his direction. "Don't even think about it."

From the ground, Ash yells, "Stop pointing that thing at my brother! Why don't you go to Old House yourself, you jerk?"

"You think I haven't tried? I've walked through those ruins dozens of times. Old House won't take me. But it'll take Garnet. I've seen it."

"You're our cousin!" Ash exclaims. "How can you do this?"

Brand's eyes are cold. "Tana is your cousin too. Have you spared any thought for her?" He motions with the gun. "Little boy. Get over there next to your brother."

Oak clenches his fists and walks stiff-legged to Ash.

"Stop pointing the gun at them," I beg Brand. "I'll do what you say."

"Garnet, no!" Ash exclaims.

I don't have a choice. This man is armed and crazed. He could pick me up and throw me through the gate if he wanted to.

Besides, I feel the pull of the place now. The creepy sensation that warned me away is fading, replaced by a strange attraction. Windy's augury showed me passing through the pillars of the old gate and vanishing. And Jasper's sly expression when he booted me from his room this morning…did he sense, as heir to the Carrefour magic, that the time had come for me to fulfill my destiny? *A sturdy girl,* he called me on our first meeting when he stole life energy from me. *You'll do just fine.*

What about Tana? Jasper claimed she'd been warned not to come here, but what if it was the opposite? What if he encouraged her to take a closer look at the house she could sometimes see? Who knows how many people he's sent here deliberately?

But maybe, for me, it won't turn out the way he expects. When I walked through the sliding glass door in Crossroad House, I saw an abandoned pool turned into a sparkling oasis. When I climbed the attic stairs last night, I met two long-dead children. Both times, I returned to the present unharmed. What if Windy's augury—which sent my mother fleeing—was only a glimpse of one of my time-walking episodes? What if it was never a threat at all?

I walk toward the stone columns.

"Garnet!" Ash hollers.

"Shut up," Brand growls.

It's like their voices belong to people I don't know, speaking about things that have nothing to do with me. Gripping the bear talisman around my neck, I brush my fingers against the nearest stone pillar. I hear no warning from my talisman, feel no urge to stop. Someone calls out my name again, but I don't look to see who it is.

Instead I walk through the gateless gate to Old House.

25

Bloodstone

Color: *deep green with crimson spots*

Magical properties: *protects from evil attack and intruders*

To recharge: *place in direct sunlight*

The gray daylight vanishes, like someone hit a switch. The air wraps me in warmth and humidity. I'm time-walking and I've left a cold autumn morning for summer, nighttime, and some long-ago year.

A cobblestone driveway stretches ahead of me, flanked by a well-tended lawn. My feet wobble in the crevices between the stones because I'm no longer wearing sneakers with soft soles. The tips of leather boots peek from beneath a skirt with a frilly hem. I know who this must be. I recognize her stride and fashion from last night in the nursery.

Clouds shift away from the pale moon, illuminating the manor house ahead.

Rose said: *If either of you ever see Old House...run as fast as you can in the opposite direction.* But that's not an option for a time-walker in someone else's head.

The main part of the house is three stories high. Two wings branch off, each of them one-story. The windows look tightly shut, which seems strange in the age before air conditioning, but if my history teacher was right, people in the 1800s would've sweltered in their beds before sleeping with open windows. They thought night air made you sick.

It isn't the stillness of the house that strikes me as wrong. It's something else. I think the girl whose body I inhabit senses it too. She stops and gazes at the treetops.

Leaves rustle, making a gentle *swish-swish* sound. But there's no wind to stir them.

My booted feet take me to the front steps, where my host diverts to the right, walking along the exterior of the house. The first floor is five feet above the ground, with windows a bit higher than that, so she can't see through them. Only when she comes to the adjacent one-story wing are the windows at ground level. The moonlight reflects an image of a girl with bronze-colored hair, a confident gaze, and arched eyebrows.

Just as I suspected. This is Stella Carrefour, looking younger than Jasper's photograph of her. Closer to my twelve years than River's sixteen.

Old House burned down before Stella was born. If she's seeing it intact, she's time-walking, like she was when she visited her siblings.

Does that mean I'm safe? Stella leaves this place and grows up to raise four children. She won't be trapped here, and if I'm riding with her, does that mean I'll leave too?

While I consider that hopeful possibility, Stella notices something less comforting. With an exclamation, she pushes through the shrubbery and plucks a strange object from a windowsill.

Made of straw and bound with twine, it has four limbs, a short torso, and a stubby head. To me, it looks like a crude, handmade doll, but to Stella it must mean something sinister. She drops it and mangles it with the heel of her boot.

Pushing her way through the shrubbery and tearing her skirt in the process, Stella strides to the next window. She plucks a doll from that windowsill and a third from the one after that, demolishing each in turn. Her eyes fix on the trees again. Their upper branches dance fitfully, as if caught in a windstorm, while the air around them remains unnaturally still. About fifty yards away from us stands a brick building that probably serves as a carriage house, considering how the cobblestone drive leads right up to it.

Somebody is behind that building. A voice mutters in a low pitch, the indistinct words followed by a *crack* that sets Stella's teeth on edge. As she creeps toward the carriage house, the air tingles with magic, like we're close to high-voltage wires. When she reaches the corner of the building and peers around it, her breath catches. "No!"

A man stands over a tree stump in the yard. Judging by the nearby stack of firewood, the stump is regularly used as a chopping block. Now it serves as a tabletop for a spell.

Four black candles squat inside a circle of stones, like points on a compass. Close to the center there's a basin of water with an incense burner rising out of it. A tendril of smoke spirals into the sky. Beside the basin, a bundle of sticks forms a miniature pyre, upon which stands another straw doll.

All the earth powers are represented in this spell, but there's something drastically wrong with the way they're being used. Black candles don't make good magic. My mom hates them so much that when she sees them in a store, she buys them and destroys them so mundanes won't accidentally summon dark forces into their lives. The stones are too far away to identify by sight, but I know them by their song of protection. They're bloodstones, like the one in the bracelet I brought from home. But the man raises a hammer and smashes them.

Bloodstones are used only for protection. Breaking them is like shooting a unicorn. My mind flinches as each song is snuffed out. Stella's body reacts right along with me.

The man surveys his handiwork, tossing the hammer to the ground. The moon lights his face, startling me. It's Old Linden, of course, but he's not old. I do the math: he was born in 1874; the house burned in 1892. He would've been eighteen.

This "Old" Linden Carrefour is a dumb kid, and he's about to do something very bad.

"In the name of the Carrefour family," he intones, "and by the power rising from this primordial crossroad, I call for the destruction of those who have taken our home. In payment for this service, I offer the sacrifice of my firstborn son."

"No!" Stella cries, plunging forward. "Stop!"

Linden whirls to face her, his arm springing up, extended in her direction. For the second time in my life, I'm facing a gun—an old-fashioned model with a long barrel that is no less terrifying than its modern counterpart.

"Papa!" Stella puts her hands up in automatic but useless defense.

Linden freezes. "Who are you?"

"Papa, don't you know me?" She must realize he *can't* know her, and still, by her voice, she is shocked.

So is he. The barrel of the gun drops until it's pointed at the ground. He stares at her like he's seeing a ghost, which he is, in a reverse sort of way.

"Don't do this," Stella chokes out. "It's a great evil, and it won't turn out the way you think. It's a perversion of earth power, to curse the people in this house. It's a *defilement*."

Linden surveys Stella with a shifting expression. "It is not done lightly, but if *you* exist—if you are my daughter and in possession of Carrefour gifts so that you walk among the paths of time—then I am destined to succeed. It is a worthy sacrifice: one child for the future of our family."

"No! Please, let me tell you—" She steps forward.

"Stay back!" Linden throws up a hand, and Stella stops moving as if blocked by an invisible wall. "It is better not to know too much about one's future." He makes a gesture, like Windy and River do when controlling air and water, and the miniature pyre on the tree stump goes up in flames. "My firstborn child," Linden promises, "for the deaths of the interlopers."

The wrongness I've been feeling since my arrival swells and crashes over me. Earth elements must want to participate for a spell to work, but those bloodstones have had their magic ripped from them, and the rest—the water corrupted by greasy incense, the burning straw doll—are being forced to work in ways that aren't natural.

Stella sinks to her knees in what feels like equal parts nausea and grief, her eyes fixed on the effigy that now represents *both* of her siblings.

Linden misspoke. *My firstborn son.* Then, *My firstborn child.* They're not the same person. When will he realize his mistake? When Ruby is born first?

Horror and grief hit me, some of it backwash from Stella, some of it my own. That over-the-top nursery packed with toys was a manifestation of Linden's guilt. And teaching the children defensive wards—was that some fruitless attempt to combat his own curse? Stella must have guessed the truth when she visited them. Or maybe she already knew. I don't know where these time-walking voyages fall within Stella's personal timeline.

At this moment, Linden shows no sign of whatever guilt he'll someday feel. His expression is unrepentant in the flickering light of the fire. "Until we meet in the due course of time, you must be gone, girl." His eyes narrow, and he peers at Stella more intently. "*Both of you,* specters from the future, be gone!"

He sees me!

Linden blows vigorously across the burning pyre of twigs, sending a cloud of ash in our direction.

Something yanks at me, like a fishhook catching my soul. The scene of Linden's horrible violation of earth magic shrinks into the distance, and everything goes black.

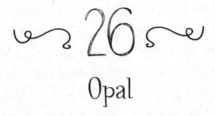

Opal

Color: *translucent with interior colors*

Magical properties: *aides in channeling psychic journeys*

To recharge: *rub between fingers, wear against the skin*

I float on a rising tide of nausea. It's like being back on the car ride to Crossroad House. Maybe everything since then was a dream, lived in mere seconds while asleep in that car.

But even if I conjured my relatives out of imagination, there's no way I could have invented Old Linden Carrefour sneaking like a thief onto the property of Old House to curse its inhabitants and pledge his future children as payment.

Opening my eyes, I blink up at a white ceiling with ornamental molding. To my right, there's an elegant staircase of polished dark wood. On my left is a wall of gleaming white paneling punctuated by pewter fixtures with glass globes and gas flames.

This isn't one of the decrepit hallways of Crossroad House. This must be Old House.

Clutching my stomach, I sit up and see not Stella's skirts and heeled boots, but my own two legs dressed in sneakers and jeans. I'm here in body, not merely in spirit.

Did closer proximity to the crossroad of ley lines give me more control over my time-walking? Or was it my ancestor Linden Carrefour, casting me and Stella out of his time period? Whichever the case, my gift has leveled up.

I scramble to my feet, and the soft squeak of my sneakers on the marble floor doesn't break the silence so much as die within it. This house swallows the sound. Sluggishly, I turn in a circle, getting my bearings. I know *where* I landed... but *when*?

A door with a glass arch window above looks like the main entrance to the house. At the opposite end of the hallway there's a set of double doors leading farther into the house, one of which is slightly ajar. I look back and forth between the two options.

It should be the exterior door for the win. So why can't I bring myself to move in that direction?

If I exit the house, I might end up safely in my own time, like that judge did. Safe, if you don't count Brand waiting by the ruined gate with a gun on Ash and Oak. And we'll never know for sure what happened to Tana.

Mom would want me to run like heck for that front door.

Instead I turn toward the double doors. My heart flutters erratically, but I have to at least peek.

Not because of Brand and his gun.

Because Tana was my cousin.

It's not an easy decision. Every step toward those double

doors feels like slogging through hip-deep slime. In spite of its immaculate appearance, there's something *wrong* with this house, the same kind of wrongness that cried out from the elements in Linden's spell.

I hear no stone songs, although the floor is made of marble, and expensive crystals hang from the chandelier. The garnet lying against my throat is silent. When I reach into my pocket to rub the onyx stones together, I can't hear their hum or the scratch of stone on stone. Even the sound of my footsteps is stolen by this beautiful, horrible house.

A gentle push on one of the double doors reveals a second hallway running perpendicular to the foyer. Directly across from me is another partially open door. On the floor of that room, a soup tureen lies overturned on its side.

Like the judge described in 1915.

I shuffle one step forward, and then another, until I can peer through the half-open doorway.

There are dead bodies in the dining room. Draped across the table and prostrate on the floor. A kitchen maid is sprawled between an Oriental rug and the dining room wall, less than two feet from me. Her hand curls around the tureen lid, the skin brown and shriveled.

I gag, but there's nothing in my stomach to bring up.

A voice in my mind whispers, *Get out of here!* But my fear is muffled, like the sounds in this house. *Not until I confirm she's here.* I poke my head into the room. There's no gore, no flies, no smell. It's almost possible to pretend the bodies are dummies in a haunted house attraction. Gritting my teeth, I pretend very hard, and look for details.

Six people have collapsed in their chairs, and three

more are crumpled on the floor. Poison jumps to mind because they were seated for a meal, but then, how did the servants die?

What did Linden's spell *do*?

The McArdle family did not die in their sleep the night he cast his spell. They died at some unspecified time after that, in the middle of their supper. Perhaps Linden poisoned the house itself, the toxicity sinking into the walls and floors, eventually overtaking the inhabitants all at once, and then...wiping the evidence off the face of the earth?

This house burned to the ground, but no bodies were found in the ruins. Why would they be? They're still here. The judge and the colonel saw them too....

With a gasp, I look more closely at the servants. Two are women, and one is a man seated against the far wall. His head is tilted back, face angled toward the ceiling, eyes closed.

The female servants are wearing uniforms. This man wears a brown suit. He's not a member of the family; there's no chair for him. There's a hat on the floor by his hand, like he came in from outside.

I nod to myself. That man has to be the colonel who discovered a long-gone house full of dead people in 1915.

I push the door open farther, but it only moves a couple of inches before meeting resistance.

Holding my breath, steeling myself, I look behind the door.

Here, at last, is Tana Kostopoulos.

She's curled in the corner, her face hidden behind waves of silky, dark hair. One of her hands is pressed against the door as if in supplication.

Flashes of cold wash over me. I can't get enough air. Leaning against the door, I breathe in and out, gradually reducing my ragged gasps to long pulls. When I'm sure I'm not going to pass out, I look at Tana again. She's dressed in shorts, a tank top, and the flip-flops I know well. Her long legs don't look mummified, like the other victims in the room, but when I force myself to bend down and touch one, the skin feels cool and dry.

I know now. It's enough. Time to flee this mausoleum.

Tearing my gaze from the girl on the floor, I turn to leave and flinch in shock. The door is shut, and I'm staring at it from *inside* the dining room. How did that happen? I never stepped over the threshold, and I didn't shut the door!

Never mind how you got in here. Get out now.

The door handle doesn't turn. Pawing at it, I search for a push-button lock or a little dial that turns. But it's a plain crystal knob. There isn't a keyhole. Why would it have one? This is a dining room! I scrabble at the crack between the door and the frame with my fingernails and pound on the door with my fists.

None of which does me any good at all.

27

Aquamarine

Color: *pale blue*

Magical properties: *brings agents for guidance and protection*

To recharge: *tumble with hematite*

I look for another way out. The windows.

Darting around the bodies, I pull aside heavy drapes, unlatch the bottom window sash, and heave upward. Like the door, it won't budge.

Desperation overcomes squeamishness. I push one of the dead bodies out of his seat. He falls woodenly, and I lift the chair. It's heavy, but I heave it at the window. It hits and bounces off, taking me down on the rebound.

I pick myself up—and the chair—and throw it again. Why won't the glass break? The third time, my arms shake, and I stumble backward more than I manage to throw the chair forward, landing in a trembling heap on the carpet.

Why didn't I run for the front door when I had the chance? What misguided confidence made me think I could stick my head in this room and still get away?

"Hello?"

Mom, I'm sorry. You were afraid I'd be another victim of this place, and that's exactly what I've become.

"Girl, can you hear me? Wake up!"

The words sound like they're coming from the bottom of a pool. Or, maybe, I'm the one in the pool, and the speaker is warm and dry in the sunlight. I open my eyes to find that I'm lying facedown on the floor. Between the legs of chairs and the table and the limbs of bodies still seated for dinner, I see two feet in black leather shoes near the doorway.

I almost scream, considering this is a room full of dead people. But the feet are *outside* the dining room, and the door is open. I lurch clumsily upright, colliding with the table.

"Take care! That room will disorient you every way it can."

I blink, focusing. "Stella?"

She stands beyond the threshold, looking a few years older than the night Old Linden cast his spell. Her skirt is less frilly. Her hair is bobbed below her jaw. "Do you know me?"

"Someone showed me your photograph." I grope my way around the table, and when I let go to maneuver around bodies, I end up on my hands and knees again. The pattern of the rug swims crazily. My eyes close against the confusion.

"Wake up!" Something strikes my head.

"Ow!" A tapered wax candle rolls back and forth in front of my nose. "Did you throw a candle at me?"

For answer, another candle hits me in the head. "What's your name?"

"Garnet." I rub my head.

"Listen, Garnet! I can't enter the room, or I'll be trapped too." Stella squats, lowering her face to my level. "This place is like a pitcher plant, enticing its prey to walk in willingly. Once inside, the sticky nectar makes it hard for victims to move while they're being dissolved and eaten. You don't want to be eaten by this nasty old house, do you, Garnet?"

A third wax taper bounces off my face. "Stop that!" I holler.

"I'm out of candles, so the next thing I throw will be the pewter bases. I failed to get the colonel out of there—he didn't believe I was real, kept calling me a tormenting spirit—and I never forgave myself. I'm not letting you die too. Start moving!"

I try. This time, I crawl. Hands. Knees. Shuffling.

"Tell me, who showed you my photograph?"

Who is this jabbering person? Oh, right. Stella. "My great-grandfather," I mutter.

"Your great-grandfather? Oh dear. That sounds like it might be a long way from my time. Why did your great-grandfather show you my photograph?"

"We're both time-walkers."

"You're a Carrefour? I should have guessed, by your name. You're doing very well. Don't put your head down, Garnet!" Stella's voice grows sharp, the way one might expect of a great-great-grandmother. "Keep moving, or I shall throw this pewter thing, and it will leave a very big lump indeed."

"It's too far." *Mom, I'm sorry, but Stella is yards and yards away, and the house wants me to stay right here.*

"You're closer than you think. Keep moving."

It would be so much *easier* to lie with my face against the rug and my heart over the ley lines in the earth beneath me. In fact, I think I'll do just that.

"The girl in the corner," Stella snaps. "Is she still alive?"

I blink. *Tana.* "No."

"Are you sure? The last time I was here, she was weak, but not completely gone."

I lift my head to gape at the girl in the doorway. Stella left Tana here to die?

Stella meets my gaze steadily. "I couldn't reach her without crossing the threshold, and I couldn't convince her to move. I keep coming back to try again. Sometimes the door is closed. Sometimes it's open, trying to entice me in. Sometimes it closes while I'm here, to keep what it has. That's why you must *keep moving*!"

I slap one hand down after the other, dragging my knees like a baby.

"Atta girl! We time-walkers don't go down easily! That's why you're going to grab that girl as you pass by and pull her out with you."

What? I can hardly drag myself, let alone a dead body!

"You can do it," Stella urges me. "Her leg is right there."

She's right. My fingers close on Tana's bare leg. *Cold. Too cold.* Her body isn't stiff, like the corpse I pushed out of the chair, but she's limp and unwieldy. "I need help!"

"As soon as you bring her over the threshold, I can help."

Straining to drag Tana from behind a door that might close any second, I complain about doing it all by myself.

Stella cheerfully agrees and badgers me to move faster. With a groan, I turn away from the doorway. Taking my eyes off the goal is torture, but it's the only way I can haul Tana—sitting on my butt and scooting backward.

I imagine the silent diners mock me from the table. *Do you think you're leaving? That's only a game the house likes to play, letting victims think they're getting away.*

Hands grab me, and I shriek. But it's Stella. She hauls me bodily over the threshold, and the fogginess in my brain drifts away. I look and see that the candles Stella threw at my head lie no more than ten feet away. Why did it take so long to crawl ten feet?

"Ha!" Stella shouts triumphantly toward the walls. "No match for a pair of Carrefour girls, are you? I got her out on the first try!"

I don't think it's a good idea to taunt the house, especially when Tana's not out of the room. "This girl is a Carrefour too." Caught in a tangle of legs, only one third of which are my own, I grab the belt loops on Tana's shorts. Stella hooks her hands under my armpits. We heave.

The door closes. "No!" I scream.

"Yes! We have her! Look!"

I shake the last of the cobwebs from my head.

The door is closed, and Tana is on *this* side with Stella and me.

28

Blue Fluorite

Color: *blue or violet*

Magical properties: *clears the mind of distractions and psychic manipulation*

To recharge: *warm between your hands*

Stella rolls Tana onto her back. Hair falls away from the girl's face, and I wince at the gray cast to her skin. Hollows rim her eyes, and her chapped lips are colorless. She looks dead.

But Stella presses an ear against her chest and grins. "She's breathing."

Impossible! "She's been gone so long! Over twenty years!"

"You must be new to time-walking." Stella jumps up. "Feet or head?"

"Uh…" It takes my brain a second to catch up to her meaning. "Feet?" Stella hooks her elbows under Tana's armpits. I grab her ankles, and together we stand.

But twenty years…and not dead? "Is there anyone else

in this house? There are supposed to be others." A university student vanished from the archaeology expedition about nine months before I was born. "Is there a young person dressed like I am?" Jeans, T-shirt, sneakers...what a college student would be wearing in the early 2010s.

Stella's eyes go immediately to the staircase, as if recognizing my description. "There are people all over this house. The dining room is the worst, but there are traps everywhere. No one alive. Only this girl. And you."

"But this person came here *after* Tana!"

"Time doesn't pass normally in this house." Stella shuffles backward, carrying Tana. "Most victims go quickly, like a candle snuffed out. This girl is an exception, and if she's a Carrefour, that's probably why."

Hobbling forward, trying to keep Tana's body from dragging on the floor, I glance over Stella's shoulder and gasp. Ahead are the double doors leading to the dining room. "We're going the wrong way!"

"We're not! Look at me. I promise not to play tricks on you."

Tearing my gaze away from that vile doorway, I concentrate on Stella's face. *What if she's the trick?* What if I'm lying on the dining room floor, dreaming of my escape while Old House dissolves me into goo?

"Garnet, focus your mind!" Stella snaps. "The house still has a hold on you. This girl needs medical attention. My father can help, although it's not his specialty."

"Your evil father, who created this evil place?"

"How do you know—" Stella catches herself and replies, "My father isn't evil. Although he did an evil thing."

The door behind Stella has hazily re-formed into the front entrance of the house. We *are* headed in the right direction, as long as I don't look directly at it. "In my time, there's a houseful of people who can care for her—and a brother waiting. We should take here there."

"Do you know how to take her back to your time?"

My expression gives away my answer because she follows up briskly. "I can give you pointers after we've passed the front door. I'm sure she'd rather see her brother than my father. What I don't understand is why this girl wandered into Old House dressed in her undergarments."

She means Tana's shorts and tank top. "That isn't underwear. It's the way people dress in her time."

Stella makes an *eeek* face. "It's a bit shocking!"

"I bet people said the same when you bobbed your hair," I shoot back.

"Touché!"

Stella bumps against the front door and lowers Tana carefully to the floor. "Navigating home without any side trips is difficult until you get accustomed to it, and it'll be even more challenging for three of us traveling together." She swings the front door open and steps through. "The first thing you must keep in mind is..."

I wipe my sweaty hands, one at time, while still supporting Tana's legs. "The first thing you must keep in mind is what?"

No answer.

"Stella?" Gooseflesh ripples down my arms. I stick my head outside without letting go of Tana.

Stella is gone.

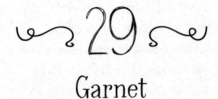

Garnet

Color: *many varieties, but most famously dark red*

Magical properties: *bolsters self-esteem, courage, and hope; protects travelers*

To recharge: *place in hot water*

I half drag, half roll Tana out of the house. My stomach sinks when I see that Stella didn't step just out of sight. Between one word and the next she vanished, leaving me like a doomed insect that clawed its way out of the pitcher plant only to find itself inside another, larger pitcher plant.

I hoped to be instantly transported back to my own time. But instead of standing among ruins, I'm on the front stoop of the house surrounded by a layer of damp fog so thick, I can barely glimpse the cobblestone driveway at the bottom of the steps. Behind me, the door to Old House gapes open. Gaslit sconces line the bright, clean entrance hall. *Safer here,* the house seems to whisper. *Bring her back inside where it's warm.*

"You'd like that, wouldn't you?" I say out loud. But what can I do instead?

Stella, I need you! If she's able to return, I'm sure she will, but I can't stand around waiting. Tana doesn't have that kind of time, and I might not either.

The gate brought me here; maybe it will take me home. It seems like an overwhelming task to drag Tana that far, but what choice do I have? Staring down the steep front steps, I can think of only one way to get her to the bottom. "Let's get to know each other," I say with fake cheer, sitting on the top step with my legs around the girl like we're sharing a sled. "I'm Garnet Carrefour, and you're Tana Kostopoulos, though really, you're a Carrefour."

Even in this position, Tana is more of a life-sized rag doll than a person. Dead weight. *Stop thinking that!* "Your mother and my great-grandfather are siblings," I go on. "We're about the same age right now, though we didn't start out that way. You've met my mother, Emerald, if that gives you some idea who I am."

Bump, slide, bump. Grab Tana's shoulders and stop her from falling sideways.

"I met your brother," I grunt, already panting from the effort. "Not a fan. I know he's trying to save you. But he waved a *gun* in my face!"

When we reach the cobblestones, I sling Tana's arm over my shoulder and try to stand, but her weight pulls me back down. "This works in the movies," I grumble, thinking of scenes where someone half carries an unconscious friend away from disaster that way. "Sorry, I'll have to drag you." Better on grass than cobblestones, so I haul her off the driveway and onto the lawn.

Then, walking backward, I pull her into the fog.

Thick white murk swallows us like a snake snapping up a pair of field mice. My back and shoulders immediately start to ache. To get my mind off the pain, I tell Tana how I learned about the Carrefours through Mom's stories: summers by the pool, snow forts in the winter, cousins opening Christmas presents together in the front parlor of Crossroad House. "Was it like that for you, Tana? Did your mother tell you so much about her family that you and Brand had to come see for yourselves?"

Tana has no answer.

I stop to catch my breath. How much farther? The fog is so opaque, I can't see the cobblestone road anymore. It's like the earth elements themselves are conspiring against me. What is fog but water and air? Not my area of expertise, but I doubt even Windy and River could disperse this murky soup with a wave. Keeping hold of Tana's hand—I think letting go of her was Stella's mistake—I sidestep to my left as far as I can go. No cobblestones.

Where's the road? I've been dragging Tana in a straight line. The fog distorts everything, but there's a looming shape behind me that might be Old House—and another one ahead that also might be Old House. It's trying to trick me. Which direction is the gate? Is *any* direction toward the gate?

Sinking to my knees in the wet grass, I stifle a sob. I'm lost. This fate was cast for me before I was born, and I was doomed to suffer it the moment Brand forced me through the crumbling gateposts. My hand convulses around Tana's. *I'm sorry, cousin.*

Her hand closes around mine.

I stare at those slim fingers. Cold. Dry. Desperate. She *is* alive. Tears blur my sight. "I don't know how to get us out of here," I whisper. The fingers flutter, then go still.

It's not fair. I got her out of the horrible dining room. Stella helped, hollering from the doorway and throwing candlesticks, but it was me who did the work. Why can't I get her home?

I saw you, Brand said. *Over and over.*

He waited years for me to be born, and to be old enough to do whatever he saw me doing. He never said exactly what that was. *But he sent me to save his sister. He was desperate enough to pull a gun on children to make this happen. And in the end, I walked through the gates voluntarily. Doesn't that count for something, that I came here with intention?*

Despair and a cruel hope wrestle in my heart. I don't know how to save Tana except to drag her through the gate toward Crossroad House. Where I left her brother waiting. But I could waste the last of my strength hauling her in the wrong direction.

No match for a pair of Carrefour girls, Stella crowed at the house.

I force myself shakily to my feet. I am a Carrefour. We built Old House to harness the magic emanating from the intersection of ley lines. But my ancestor corrupted that magic with his vile spell. Now Tana and I are paying for it. *Dark deeds have dark consequences,* Windy's mother said when Rose suggested we help Jasper to his end. *And earth magic has a long memory.*

Unless... If Stella is right, time doesn't work normally

on the Old House grounds. Does that mean I can reach back to *before* Linden cast his evil spell?

Generations of Carrefours lived and prospered in Old House before it was lost to bankruptcy. Can I call upon the magic from *their* time, the way Mom's GPS reroutes us around a traffic jam?

Closing my eyes, I attune my senses the way Mom taught me. Outside the dampening field of Old House's treacherous rooms and hallways, the garnet pendant rediscovers its voice, roaring its vow of protection. The onyx stones in my pocket hum their desire to help.

The magic Uncle Mica poured into these stones is like having my uncle walk beside me. A fragile thread of hope weaves itself into a broader ribbon of confidence when I conjure in my mind the other Carrefours I've come to know. What would River hear in the whisper of air, if she was here? What might Ash pick up, in the rustle of the grass? What would LJ learn from the trees?

Despite the gentle sounds I detect, I don't know which direction to drag my unconscious cousin. It's not fair I lost Stella before she finished the first sentence of her time-walking tutorial. *The first thing you must keep in mind...* Is what?

In *The Wizard of Oz*, Dorothy has to think of *home*. Maybe Stella was going to say: *The first thing you must keep in mind is where you are going.*

"There's no place like home," I whisper. Immediately I picture Crossroad House, with its peeling wallpaper and falling-down porch, the burned-out wing clinging to its side like a parasite. I grew up somewhere else, but Crossroad

House is home. Sure, it's dirty and crumbling, but now that I've met its bigger, eviler, older brother, I know where the trouble comes from.

I think about my cousins—Ash, who inherited Uncle Flint's love for family history, and River, standing up against Jasper to defend her grandmother. I think about LJ catching Oak like a football when he flew off the roof, and Uncle Mica forcing himself down those attic steps to sit beside me and my mom.

It's not enough. The fog thickens and the air gets colder. *Dig deeper, Garnet!*

Pressing a heel onto the back of a sneaker, I pry off one shoe and then the other. I strip off my socks, one after the other, never completely letting go of Tana. Once my feet are bare, I wiggle my toes in the wet grass. Cold. Slimy. Like a bed of juicy earthworms...

Nope. That's Old House pushing its grossness at me. This location was chosen by Diamon Carrefour for its magical potential. He built a beautiful house here. *Beautifully evil.* I shake my head. *No, not when it was built.*

How many Carrefour children have played on this lawn? Hide-and-seek. Blind man's buff. Jumping rope. *If I listen carefully, I can hear them.*

When I open my eyes, I see a speck of color in the sea of gray fog. Slipping my arms under Tana's, I drag her to that bit of color. It turns out to be a dandelion defiantly growing out of a trimmed green lawn.

I look around. There! Another one!

This time it takes more effort. My back screams in pain. All for a dandelion jutting cheerily out of pebbly dirt.

And two more beyond it.

The fog swirls, threatening to erase the bright yellow, but I dig my toes deeper into the wet grass, seeking what's beneath. My magic. My heart. *I know you're there, underneath the corruption.*

Tears stream down my face from pain as I drag Tana along the dandelion path, ignoring shadowy Old Houses trying to confuse me, until a swath of dandelions paints a path—my own yellow brick road—toward two stone pillars marking the way out of this cursed place.

Three figures wait beyond. The smallest crouches on the ground with his hands thrust into a mound of dandelions. The other two are adult-sized—Brand and someone else.

I know the exact moment I become visible to them because Ash shouts, "There she is!"

"Tana!" Brand dashes through the gateway.

I expect him to vanish, whisked away like Stella was. But Ash's dandelion path must protect him because he reaches me and scoops his sister into his arms. For a second, I hang on to her, afraid of what will happen if we're separated. "I've got her!" Brand grunts in agitation. When I see his face, I let go before it becomes a tug-of-war.

The skin around his left eye is swollen, like someone punched him. What happened while I was gone?

Brand runs back to the gateway, and I limp behind. It feels like I ran a marathon to bring Tana this far. *Leaving me an empty vessel...*

"Garnet!" My name, shouted in a rusty door hinge of a voice, snaps my head up. The other adult waiting at the pillars is Uncle Mica, down from his attic and stepping toward me.

"Stop! I'm coming!" What did it cost my uncle to leave his refuge? Enough that Old House will think him a tasty, weakened treat? I might be an empty vessel, but I know how to fill myself up. I breathe deeply. Listen. Feel the magic.

Take that, cursed house. I remember you before the curse, and now you know me, too.

I sprint the last fifty yards.

Ash grins like a maniac when I dash between the stone pillars, dandelions exploding from the ground like fluffy yellow bombs.

I run full tilt into my uncle's arms.

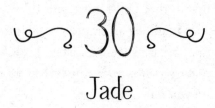

30

Jade

Color: *mid- to dark green*

Magical properties: *promotes healing and soothes family discord*

To recharge: *place among amethyst crystals overnight*

Uncle Mica heaves me onto his shoulder and carries me back to Crossroad House at a dead run. Brand sprints ahead of us with Tana. Ash trails behind, arms pumping at his sides, but his magic outpaces us. Across the neglected lawn, blooms burst open. Not just dandelions. Daffodils. Tulips. Pansies.

As we crest the hill leading from the old swimming pool, Oak runs out of the house, pointing, with Linden behind him. They stop, ankle-deep in violets, gaping at the carpet of flowers. Brand reaches them first, and Linden stares at the girl in his arms, exclaiming, "No, it *can't* be! It's impossible! I don't believe it!"

"Believe it or not," Brand gasps. "But get out of the way!"

Linden makes room for him to pass, then gawks at

who's following behind. "Mica?" Uncle Mica pushes past Linden and into the house, where I hear Mom frantically shouting my name.

"I'm okay, Mom!"

"Garnet, baby!" She claps her hands around my face. "Oak said you went through the gates of Old House and disappeared! Just like—" Her voice wobbles.

"I was time-walking."

"You were *what*?" Uncle Mica carries me into Holly's kitchen and plops me into a chair. Tana is sprawled on the table, and Holly is examining her. Mom looks back and forth between the patient and the bearded man hovering nearby. "Brand? Is that *Tana*?" Mom turns to stare at me. "What did you do?"

"She's dangerously dehydrated." Holly turns to her husband. "Take her to our bedroom. I'll need all my equipment."

Ash's dad lifts Tana off the table and elbows his way past everyone. Holly follows, and Brand tries to go too, but Linden blocks him. "*You* are staying right where you are."

Brand scowls. "I'm going with my sister." But when Linden doesn't back down—and when Uncle Mica joins him, shoulder to shoulder—Brand slumps.

"Sit," Linden snaps.

Brand collapses into the nearest chair and gingerly probes his swollen eye. Someone should give him an ice pack, but nobody does.

Linden crosses his arms. "Oak says you threatened him with a gun. Is that true? You pointed a gun at my nephews and forced Garnet onto the Old House land?"

Mom gasps out loud. Grimly, Uncle Mica pulls a gun from the back pocket of his pants and tosses it onto the table. I flinch, as do half the people in the room.

Brand says weakly, "It's a stage prop."

Mom looks like she wants to rip his throat out with her teeth. "You terrorized our children and coerced my daughter into real danger, no matter if your gun was fake."

"I knew she'd save Tana. I saw it happen in a vision."

"*A vision.*" Mom sneers, like Brand is claiming he can fly.

I speak up. "He's a Carrefour, Mom."

"Hestia's son," Ash adds.

The adults exchange incredulous glances. "Is this true?" Linden demands.

"Try and remove me from the property and see what happens," Brand replies bitterly. Then he sits up in alarm. "But not Tana! They can't take her to the hospital! It'll kill her!"

"I don't think they'd do that. How would they explain who she was? But—" Linden turns to Oak. "Warn your parents." Oak runs off.

Mom bangs her fists on the table. "What happened? What did you do to the children?"

Brand tells the same story he told me earlier. "I did what I had to do," he finishes, glancing up at Uncle Mica and Linden. "You would've done the same for your sisters."

Uncle Mica points at the fake gun and shakes his head.

"Mica walloped him good," Ash volunteers. "He showed up right after Garnet disappeared. I'm not sure how he knew what was going on."

Uncle Mica's face flushes, but after a moment he opens his mouth and croaks, "Attic window. He took the kids."

Mom grips her brother's shoulder, blinking back tears, and Linden gives him an encouraging nod before turning to me. "But how is Tana here?"

"I time-walked and brought her back."

Mom shakes her head. "You said that before. What do you mean?"

"I've been doing it since I got here. Traveling back to 1998. And 1903. Today I went back even farther. Jasper explained it to me this morning."

Expressions in the room vary. Mom's is a fleeting and terrifying *You're-in-serious-trouble-for-not-telling-me.* Linden's face flashes an alarmed *This-might-weaken-my-claim-to-be-the-next-heir.* Ash puts on a supremely innocent: *Don't-blame-me. Not-my-fault.*

I summarize what Jasper said about his mother's talent, and how I met Stella on the grounds of Old House but had to bring Tana back without her help.

"Thank you," Brand murmurs, wiping tears from his eyes with the back of his hand.

"Jasper needs to hear this," Linden declares, stalking out of the room.

Brand sighs heavily. "Can I see my sister now?"

Mom's lips curl in a snarl, like she wants to deny him. But she catches my eye and relents. "All right. I'll take you. But first..."

She pulls food out of Holly's refrigerator—cold cuts, cheese, yogurt, fruit—and addresses me and Ash. "You two, eat something. That stunt with the flowers will have overtaxed your magical energies as much as Garnet's time traveling." Her glance at me conveys an additional message: *I'm not done with you yet, missy.* Then she escorts Brand out of the room. Uncle Mica is already gone, slipped out while no one was watching.

"I don't feel overtaxed," Ash says, peeling slices of deli ham and cheese out of their packages. "I feel exhilarated. Don't you?"

I nod. That's exactly the word for it. Everything around me reverberates with music: stones, plants, water, air...I'm still marveling at the sounds other elements of earth magic can make. "Nice flowers, by the way."

"I got carried away. I was trying to reach you through the gates of Old House with a signal you'd recognize, but—" He makes an explosion gesture with his hands. "I couldn't stop. What did you do, Garnet? Besides bring Tana back. I can tell you *did* something to the magic."

I rerouted it. But that's an explanation for another time. Stuffing a slice of cheese into my mouth, I stand up. "Let's go see Tana."

❧

She looks tiny and fragile in Holly's bed. An IV is taped to the back of one hand. But her chest is rising and falling visibly.

"Come in," Holly says. "You saved her; you deserve to see her. Ash, gather some of that lavender you produced. The scent will help with her healing." She shoos Ash out of the room and slips out behind him.

I glance at Brand, slumped in a chair beside the bed.

"Tana is Greek for 'fire goddess,'" he says suddenly. "I told Windy that when we met. And *Brand* should be obvious. It was a hint about who we were."

"Not enough of a hint."

"There were other clues, if anyone had been paying attention."

Like Brand starting a fire with wet wood after Mica failed to light it. "Why didn't you tell them directly?"

"I swore to my mother I wouldn't. She didn't want us to visit Crossroad House, but neither Tana nor I was developing our aptitudes the way we should have. When I connived a way to meet Windy and get an invitation, she allowed me to take Tana on the condition that I didn't let Jasper know who we really were. I didn't think we'd even meet him because Windy said he was a bedridden invalid." He inhales harshly. "But everything went wrong. It killed my mother, you know. She died two weeks after Tana vanished. They said it was an aneurysm, but it was a broken heart. My fault."

Poor Tana. When she wakes up, she's going to discover twenty years have disappeared in a flash and her mother is gone. I lay my fingertips on her arm. The skin is warmer now, and as I pull back my hand, her eyes fly open.

I gasp, and Brand lurches to his feet. But the girl's gaze is fixed on me. "Garnet?" Her voice is a raspy croak, worse than Uncle Mica's. "Are you Garnet?"

My mouth falls open. How does she know my name?

"I heard you," she whispers. "Talking to me..."

Brand grabs his sister's arm. "Tana!" When she sees the

man standing over her, she recoils and tries—weakly—to scoot away from him. "It's me! Brand!"

Holly rushes into the room carrying a poultice that's probably meant for Brand's swollen eye. "No, darling! Stay still!" She tosses the poultice aside and puts her hands on Tana's shoulders. "Please lie down. You're safe." While Tana stares at her with bewildered eyes, Holly tries to explain. "I'm Holly Carrefour. You know me. This is your brother. You're recovering from a terrible experience and very weak."

Tana's gaze darts between Holly and Brand in growing alarm. Finally she turns to me. "Am I—like them?"

I realize what she means. Snatching up a hand mirror from Holly's dresser, I hold it in front of her face. "I'm not old," she whispers in relief.

"No," I agree. "You're not."

Holly, checking the IV line, sniffs. "*Old* is a bit unfair."

Tana looks again at her brother. "Brand?" He nods, grabs her hand, and cries over it.

A commotion outside the room makes both me and Holly stare at the doorway, muttering in unison, "What now?"

Mom sticks her head in. "It's Jasper. He's collapsed."

It makes sense. Jasper has been stealing life energy from family members for decades, and Old House has been a life-energy trap for over a hundred years, supplementing the power of the heir. To lose me and Tana at the same time must have been a blow to Jasper, and probably to the curse itself.

The next morning, Jasper summons the family to gather in the library for what everyone assumes will be his final words. He refuses to do it from a deathbed and insists Linden and LJ carry him down to his favorite chair in the library. Even in his last straits, he demands his dignity.

I choose to wait in the sunroom where I can admire Ash's flowers, still in riotous bloom. I'm not there long before Ash joins me, yawning. "Feeling sleepy?" I ask. "*Today?*" I was almost too excited to sleep last night and woke up early this morning.

Ash sits on a chair next to me. He has an envelope in his hand. "I stayed up late looking through the box Flint kept on Stella. There's nothing in there about her time-walking gift, only about her talent with all forms of earth power. He does note that she might have had some power of divination based on the story about predicting the earth talents of each of her children. But you know what I think? I don't think she predicted them at all."

I grin. "She did a little time-strolling and *peeked*." What a very Stella thing to do! "Well, Jasper knew about her time-walking and so did Hestia, according to Brand. But maybe she did less of it as she got older."

"She lived an interesting life," Ash says. "She was a suffragette, and she spent time in jail for protesting—not just for women's suffrage but also in the sixties for civil rights. There's a ton of stuff you'll want to see."

"Including that envelope?"

"It was in the bottom of the box." He hands me the yellowed envelope. Written across it, in long, elegant handwriting, are instructions.

To be read only by Garnet Carrefour
No matter how long that takes

I take it reverently from his hands. He fidgets. "If you want to read it privately..."

"No! I want you to see what's in it." The envelope is sealed with wax, which breaks apart. I ease out thick vellum paper and lean close to Ash so he can read along with me.

Dearest Garnet,

How very vexing it was to be rudely interrupted today by the whims of forces greater than ourselves—and before I gave you my promised advice! I do not know when we shall meet again, or if at all, although I hope today's excursion was not our only mutual adventure. Nevertheless, in the event our paths do not cross again, it seems prudent that I commit to paper all I have learned about our rare gift, including, most importantly, how to gain a measure of control over time traveling. Although I must warn you, it is not very precise and always a surprise in some way.

There follows, in Stella's breezy style, two pages of advice on how to develop and refine the gift of time-walking. I barely have the chance to scan the letter before River sticks her head in the door.

"It's time," she says.

ᔇ 31 ᔇ

Blue Diamond

Color: *clear with a blue tone*

Magical properties: *intensifies inner strengths, amplifies ambition, fosters rebirth*

To recharge: *diamonds need to be cleaned, not recharged*

Most of the family has already gathered, and the rest come in immediately behind us. Remembering the last time we were in this room with Jasper, I plan on staying by the door, ready to bolt if he starts cursing people. But Ash and I are shoved through the crowd and up toward the front, facing Jasper.

I suck in my breath.

In the hours since I saw him yesterday morning, Jasper has aged years. His face is reduced to ridges and hollows. Shaggy eyebrows hang over sunken eyes like shrubbery on the edge of a cliff. The Carrefour ring flops sideways on his skeletal finger as he clenches and unclenches the arm of his chair. Even his hair has deserted him—rats on a sinking ship.

The one thing unchanged is his smoldering eyes. They rake the room, beginning with Windy's mother, who started recovering from yesterday's illness as soon as Tana and I emerged from the Old House gates. Today she's well enough to sit up in a chair and looks healthier than Jasper does.

Jasper glowers next at my mom's generation, lingering slightly on Brand and Uncle Mica, who enters no farther than the doorway. When Jasper scans my generation, he snaps, "Where's that girl brought back from being twenty years dead?"

"Too weak to leave her bed, Uncle Jasper," Holly replies.

"The entire family's meant to be here."

"If you insist, I'll get Flint's wheelchair out of storage and—"

"You've made your point. Be quiet." Jasper fumes, mumbling. "It's not like I'm going to pass the power on to her, or to her idiot brother who crept around my house like a sneak thief."

Brand's eyes flame, but Jasper ignores him. "The rest of you aren't much better." He points a shaky finger at Windy. "Aptitude wasted on fortune-telling." Then Holly. "Potential squandered on the weak." His eyes scrape Linden. "Or bootlicking. Then I've got the runaway..." *(Mom.)* "...the complainer..." *(Rose.)* "...and most pitiful, the hermit from the attic."

Uncle Mica crosses his arms and leans against the doorframe, unmoved by the insult.

"Some of the youngsters have more gumption than

the lot of you." Jasper scowls at me for a long, horrifying moment.

He...wouldn't...would he?

With a sneer, he looks away. "But what do children know about keeping the family power? None of you grasp what it takes, so I'll have to make the best of a bad lot and name Linden my heir."

The statement is so anticlimactic, no one reacts at first. Then Windy makes an angry, hissing sound. After his spiteful rant, Jasper made the choice everyone expected.

Linden steps forward, straightening his oversized glasses. "I understand the trust you're placing in me, Uncle Jasper. I won't let you down."

Jasper grumbles inaudibly and eases the Carrefour ring over his swollen finger joints. The ring is begrimed again, which must be a manifestation of Jasper's crumbling life energy. Holding the ring between his fingers, he gazes avariciously at it. Linden, more confident now, holds out his hand. When Jasper doesn't drop the ring into his palm, Linden pulls it from the old man's grasp.

The shriek I hear is so blood-curdling, I throw both hands over my ears. So does Mom. Uncle Mica flinches. Nobody else in the room reacts, and it takes me a second to understand that the sound didn't come from Jasper.

It came from the Carrefour diamond.

Linden might not have heard the stone's cry, but he gasps and flings his hand open like he's holding a hot coal. The ring drops to the floor, bounces once, and rolls in a lopsided circle across the wooden floorboards before wobbling to a halt against someone's shoe.

Ash bends and picks it up. With a helpful smile, he holds it out to his uncle.

Linden stares at Ash. So does everyone else.

Ash is oblivious. "Uncle Linden, take it." He waggles his eyebrows as if to say *Everyone's watching!*

Linden looks tempted. He even twitches toward it before opening his hand to show Ash the blistering imprint left by the stone. "I can't."

"But—" Ash frowns at the ring. He's holding it between his thumb and forefinger and now allows it to drop into his palm, where it rests comfortably.

And purrs. I swear, it purrs.

"Put it on, Ash." Uncle Mica's voice is thick and grating. People who didn't hear him speak yesterday spare him an astonished glance before turning back to the other miracle happening.

Ash looks frozen. "I can't," he whispers.

Looking around, I think a lot of the adults are thinking the same thing. Windy eyes the ring with speculation. Nobody but me and Mom and Uncle Mica hears the ring itself.

Ash scans the crowd, seeking his mother. She has her hands over her mouth, her eyes wide, but after a moment of hesitation she nods. Only then does Ash slip the ring onto his finger. It's way too big for him. He looks like a kid playing dress-up.

Rose screams. Ash jumps nearly a foot in the air and whips around to face his aunt, who grabs him with both her hands and kisses him on the forehead. "I can see!" she exclaims, her eyes shining. "You wonderful boy, I can see!"

Still, Ash stands there, his hand with the ring hanging in midair like a girl who just got engaged. He turns slowly to see Jasper's reaction to his heir being rejected by the Carrefour magic itself.

Jasper hasn't reacted. His hands are in his lap. His head is pitched forward.

He's gone.

Windy's mother whispers something that might be a prayer or maybe just a heartfelt goodbye to her uncle. Everyone else exhales, and now that the ordeal is finally over, the tension in the room dissipates. For about two seconds.

A terrible crack rattles the house, followed by the sound of splintering wood. The wall with the bricked-up entrance to the burned-down wing shudders.

Uncle Mica bolts from the room, followed by LJ, and then almost everyone else in a grand smash-up, trying to fit through the door. Windy's mother stays put, her hands clasped in vigil over Jasper's body. Every other Carrefour stumbles out the front door and around the side of the house to watch the remains of the burned wing collapse in a cascade of rotted wood.

If I was in charge, the first thing I'd do is pull down that burned wing and put in a garden. That's what Ash told me the day he gave me a tour of the house and grounds.

The last blackened beam falls to the ground with a thump. Dust hovers in the air.

"I—I—" Ash stammers incoherently, looking terrified. "I can't be..."

Holly's face crumples as if she regrets giving him permission to put on the ring, and the other adults' expressions mirror Ash's own assessment. Uncle Mica is an exception, and so is Rose. But LJ is the one who puts a hand on Ash's shoulder and says, "Yes, you can! You're a fantastic choice." I can't help but notice he avoids his father's eyes, but if one thing can be said for LJ, it's that he's always sincere.

I'm more surprised by River. "You better be," she says, marching over to stand with the new heir. Her black eyes are healing while we watch. "Everybody's counting on you."

Oak approaches, his hands clenched into determined little fists. "Do it right, Ash. No more slurping spider."

Ash looks at me, and I join the circle of cousins surrounding him. "Didn't I tell you, practically as soon as we met, that Crossroad House needed a gardener?"

32

Aventurine

Color: *most commonly green or blue*

Magical properties: *promotes leadership and decisiveness*

To recharge: *place on windowsill to face the dawn*

"Why me?" Ash asks for the seven hundredth time in the twenty-four hours since he accepted the ring. He'll ask it to whoever is standing nearby.

Some have no answer for him and look like they're wondering the same thing—Windy's mother, for example, and Linden.

Brand said, "Beats me, kid."

Windy offered to cast an augury for him. (He said *no thank you* and fled.)

On this, the seven hundredth occasion of his asking, I try to frame the right answer. "Because you're perfect for the job."

"But why?" We're standing in the hallway outside the kitchen, watching through the sliding glass doors as his dad and Brand disassemble pieces of the collapsed porch and haul them into the yard. "I've been looking through Flint's boxes, trying to find another example of the house or the ring choosing its own heir. I haven't come across *anything*. Uncle Linden could do this job better than me."

"Could he, though?" Linden can handle the family business interests and investments, but he doesn't look at the *house* the way Ash does—as if it's got boundless potential. "I think you're the one who sees most clearly what Crossroad House can become. It's a bonus that you love the family history and probably know the most about it, now that Uncle Flint is gone." I peer at him closely. "Do you feel different?"

"Except for this big old ring, not really." Ash gestures, and the ring flies off his finger. Again. "Ooops." He runs down the hall after it, dusts it off on his pants, and puts it back on his finger. The first time he did that, I nearly had a heart attack, thinking he'd drop dead like Jasper. But wearing the ring isn't important. Owning it is. I helped him clean it properly, and today it remains clean and sparkling, purring like a contented cat.

I watch Ash while he watches the deconstruction of the porch. He might not notice anything different about himself, but I've caught him staring at parts of the house—a warped floorboard, a mildew-stained corner, peeling wallpaper everywhere—his head tipped at an angle as if he's *listening* to a voice only he can hear. When I asked him, shortly after the burned-out wing fell down, if Old House was still a threat, hungry for victims to replace the ones who got away, he only hesitated a few seconds before shaking his head. "I don't get that sense from it. I don't sense it at all, really."

Equally important: all the Carrefours are able to leave the property now. Yesterday, Windy drove me, Ash, and Oak into town for McDonald's. We brought fries and a shake back for Tana (although we had to smuggle them past Holly, who had set a strict diet for her patient).

Since the transition of power, the entire house is bathed in a brighter light. LJ is in good spirits because his parents are taking steps to reverse their divorce. River is glued to her phone, making plans with her friends. Mom has taken charge of Jasper's funeral, just like she did for Uncle Flint, although the mood is quite different. It feels wrong to be cheerful about a funeral, even Jasper's, but it's natural to be happy the crisis has passed.

Not everyone found the changing house a desirable place to be. Rose fled that first day. She was peeling out of the driveway when Windy brought us back from McDonald's. "She didn't waste any time," Windy commented wryly.

"I'm sure she wants to see her fiancé," Ash said, hiding his hurt.

Brand also wanted to leave with Tana, but Holly talked him out of it. "What will you do if she weakens? Take her to a hospital? They'll call the police and charge you with neglect. You don't have an ID for her except a birth certificate that says she's thirty-something years old. Try to pass that off and they'll jump from neglect straight to kidnapping!"

Brand slumped. "What am I supposed to do?"

"You're welcome to stay here until we figure out how to solve her identification problem."

Brand fingered his swollen eye. "I'm not sure I *am* welcome."

"Well," Holly replied, squinting at Brand's face. "Nobody's thrilled about how you treated the children, but I bet you could work off the bad karma."

Which is how Brand ended up ripping out the porch.

"My dad's going to put in a deck with a freestanding fireplace. In the spring, we'll repair the swimming pool." Ash cleans his broken glasses, temporarily repaired with duct tape. "Next summer, we'll be hanging by the pool, like *they* used to."

I imagine it. River will be the one with all the boyfriends, and LJ will be the lifeguard. Ash will make sure Oak isn't left out the way Rose was back in the day, and with any luck, Brand will let Tana come back—assuming they ever leave.

As for me, Mom and I had a frank discussion about our future last night. "We have to leave in the next couple of days," she said. "You've missed too much school, and I need to get back to the shop. But next summer, what would you think about moving—"

"Yes," I said before she could finish. "My whole life I've wanted to live at Crossroad House with the rest of the Carrefours. The way you did."

Mom winced. "I didn't want to deprive you of the childhood I had. But it was the only way I knew to keep you safe. Withholding the details of the augury was part of that. I'm afraid I never credited you with enough magical strength to see your own way through to safety. I'm sorry. I won't underestimate you again."

"I'm sorry I sabotaged your ward. And I should have told you right away about the time traveling. Maybe together we could have figured everything out sooner and still saved Tana, but without all the..." I made a rolling motion with my hands to gloss over the fake gun, frightened kids, and Brand going full-on desperado.

"Let's make a pact to be honest," Mom said, putting an arm around my shoulders. "We work better as a team than not. So to be clear, we're going back to the apartment. You to finish the school year. Me to find someone to manage the shop—because I don't want to give it up. And then..."

"We'll move home." Here. Crossroad House.

Which is why, this morning, I point through the sliding glass door and tell Ash, "Save the goldfish pond for me. I want to help rebuild it. I'm good with stones, you know."

"You got it."

At the other end of the house, the doorbell rings. I hurry down the hall, throw open the front door, and ask the person on the other side, "Are you from the funeral home?"

The man steps backward. "What? No, I'm...I'm sorry. Is there a funeral going on?"

"Not today!" I tell him cheerfully. Then I look at him.

He's tall and broad-shouldered, casually dressed in a sweater and jeans. His complexion is a golden olive, his hair dark and curly, and his eyes are a strikingly light shade of brown. He nervously rubs a nose that's long and curved. "I've obviously come at a bad time. Sorry."

He takes another step backward, and I unglue my tongue enough to stammer, "N-no, you—you haven't. Don't go."

He smiles in an awkward *wish-I'd-never-rung-the-doorbell* way. "Does the Carrefour family still live here?"

"Yes." I touch the amulet at the base of my throat. My little garnet bear is warm and humming.

The man heaves a breath. "Okay, this is going to sound weird, but a long time ago I had a job nearby. Today, I was driving through the area, and I got this crazy idea to get off the highway, and..." He rubs the back of his neck self-consciously. "Look, does Emerald still live here?"

"Is your name David Castellano?"

His mouth falls open. "How could you possibly know—"

My heart thrumming in my chest, I open the door wider. "I think you better come in."